THE VANDERBEEKERS

LOST and FOUND

THE VANDERBEEKERS
LOST and FOUND

By Karina Yan Glaser

HOUGHTON MIFFLIN HARCOURT
BOSTON   NEW YORK

hmhbooks.com

The text was set in Stempel Garamond.
Design by Natalie Fondriest

Library of Congress Cataloging-in-Publication Data
Names: Glaser, Karina Yan, author.
Title: Vanderbeekers lost and found / by Karina Yan Glaser.
Description: Boston ; New York : Houghton Mifflin Harcourt, 2020. | Series: The Vanderbeekers ; [4] | Audience: Ages 7 to 10. | Audience: Grades 2–3. | Summary: As they look forward to the New York City Marathon in which their friend Mr. B will run, the Vanderbeeker children learn that one of their good friends is homeless.
Identifiers: LCCN 2019052304 (print) | LCCN 2019052305 (ebook) | ISBN 9780358256199 (hardcover) | ISBN 9780358255246 (ebook)
Subjects: CYAC: Family life—New York (State)—Harlem—Fiction. | African Americans—Fiction. | Neighbors—Fiction. | Friendship—Fiction. | Harlem (New York, N.Y.)—Fiction. | New York (N.Y.)—Fiction.
Classification: LCC PZ7.1.G5847 Val 2020 (print) | LCC PZ7.1.G5847 (ebook) | DDC [Fic]—dc23
LC record available at https://lccn.loc.gov/2019052304
LC ebook record available at https://lccn.loc.gov/2019052305

Manufactured in the United States of America
DOC 10 9 8 7 6 5 4 3 2
4500811058

To Team Vanderbeeker:
Ann
Ginger
Tara
Holly

I wonder how the road beyond it goes—
what there is of green glory and soft, checkered
light and shadows—what new landscapes—
what new beauties—what curves and hills
and valleys further on.

L. M. Montgomery, *Anne of Green Gables*

Sunday, October 20

Fourteen Days Until the New York City Marathon

One

Bright morning sunshine drifted through the windows of the red brownstone on 141st Street, filling the kitchen with a soft glow. Eight-year-old Hyacinth stood on a step stool, dipping thick slices of raisin bread purchased that morning at Castleman's Bakery into an egg, milk, and cinnamon sugar mixture. She wore a floral bandana wrapped around her hair and a dress she had made from two of Papa's old striped work shirts. Oliver, age eleven, was managing frying pans on three burners with measured concentration, flipping sizzling french toast. He hadn't brushed his hair in two days, so it was even wilder than normal.

Mama had already left for work at the Treehouse Bakery and Cat Café, the cookie shop she owned and operated, and Papa sat on a stool by the stove supervising while drinking coffee, serving as fire warden and occasionally washing the dishes that piled up on the counter. Six-year-old Laney sat at his feet, brushing her rabbit Paganini's ears with a sparkly doll comb. She wore pajamas, unicorn slippers, and six strands of beads around her neck.

"Hello!" called Orlando, their upstairs neighbors' grandnephew, letting himself in through the building door on the first floor. He was built like a football player and was fourteen years old, the same age as Isa and Jessie; he wore one of the nerdy science T-shirts that Jessie liked to give him on birthdays. This one said, "Never Trust an Atom, They Make Up Everything." In Orlando's arms was Billie Holiday, formerly known as New Dog, a pup with long legs and big ears that the Vanderbeekers had found outside their door that previous spring. Mr. Jeet and Miss Josie had adopted her, but the Vanderbeekers took her out for walks daily since going up and down stairs hurt Miss Josie's knees. Mr. Jeet used a wheelchair exclusively to get around these days; he rarely went out except to go to doctor's appointments.

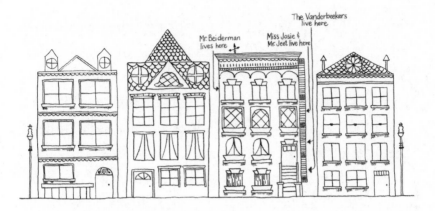

"You're spoiling that dog," Jessie said to Orlando.

He shrugged as he put Billie Holiday down. Franz ran to greet her with a low howl, and Tuxedo scampered up and batted at her ears.

"Billie Holiday doesn't like the wood stairs," Orlando said. "Too slippery."

Jessie pushed her glasses higher on her nose and turned to Isa, pointing a thumb over her shoulder toward Orlando. "See? Spoiled."

Isa gathered her long, straight hair over one shoulder and smiled. "Orlando is such a pushover when it comes to Billie Holiday."

Isa leaned down to feed George Washington, their orange tabby, while Laney scooped out a can of cat food for Tuxedo, yet another animal that had been left on their doorstep the past spring. The black-and-white kitten had been Laney's favorite of the five that had been abandoned, and she had campaigned relentlessly to keep him until her parents finally gave in. The rest of the kittens had been adopted by other families, including their friend Herman's.

Because Herman's parents did not allow pets in their home, the Vanderbeekers had coordinated for Herman's cat, who he named Purl One, to live at the cat café. Purl One, who was named after knitting terminology, was the one permanent resident; eleven other adoptable cats lived there on a rotating basis. Herman took Purl One with him whenever he could, nestling her into a kangaroo-pouch cat carrier that strapped to his chest. Hyacinth had made the carrier for him, and the Vanderbeekers agreed that Purl One was the calmest cat they had ever met. There was no way George Washington or Tuxedo would put up with that treatment.

"Get your french toast while it's hot!" Oliver called from the stove, expertly flipping a piece of perfectly browned toast onto a platter next to the burners.

Jessie grabbed the platter while Isa and Orlando

set the table. As Laney waited, she pulled the fold of her turtleneck up and chewed on it, a habit she had recently acquired. Jessie hypothesized that this new habit had a direct relationship to their neighbor Mr. Jeet's health decline over the last month. These days, Mr. Jeet spent most of his time in bed, and his periods of wakefulness had decreased significantly since the summer.

"We're going to the garden after breakfast," Jessie told Orlando. "Want to come?"

"We've got to leave food for the PM!" Laney said.

Two weeks ago, the Vanderbeekers had discovered signs that someone had been sleeping in the shed they used to store their gardening tools, soil, and seeds. They hadn't yet spotted the Person of Mystery, or PM, but hidden in a corner of the shed behind a stack of soil bags was a pile of clothes, neatly folded, plus a toothbrush, a worn Bible, and a rolled-up blanket. Worried that the PM was hungry, the kids had been leaving food next to the clothes. Each day the food was gone, so they figured whoever was staying there needed it.

Mama and Papa had been on board with the plan as long as the kids visited the garden only when there was an adult they knew inside with them. This wasn't difficult, because somebody they knew was always inside, tending their plot or taking a break from the city bustle. The gate wasn't locked at night, so the person must have been coming after dark and leaving early in the morning.

"I've been making him a scarf!" Hyacinth called to Orlando from the stove.

"I wonder who he is," Laney said. "I hope he finds a home soon."

"Yeah," Oliver agreed as he flipped another piece of french toast. "That shed is so creepy. He must be really desperate."

"If you come," Jessie said to Orlando, "you can help me record my findings." Jessie had been working on a science experiment she had started earlier that month about the effectiveness of various fertilizers. She had lined up multiple pots of mums and marked them clearly with the varying amounts of nitrogen, phosphorus, and potassium in their soil. One of them was planted in soil that had been mixed with compost made from the Vanderbeekers' food scraps and discarded hay from Paganini's litter box.

Orlando shook his head. "I've got cross-country practice."

"Is running your favorite thing to do?" Laney asked.

"Football is my favorite," Orlando said. "But our high school doesn't have a football team."

Laney looked at Orlando. "Do you like watching football?"

Orlando nodded.

"Which team are you voting for?" she asked him.

Orlando choked on a piece of french toast. "'Voting for'? Laney, if you're going to be my friend, you've got to know sports terminology. First off, you don't vote for a team. You're a *fan* of the team."

Laney swung her legs under the table. "Okay, what fan are you?"

"The Atlanta Falcons."

"Do they get a lot of home runs?" asked Laney.

Orlando clutched his heart. "Oh man, Laney, we

have a *lot* of work to do. Tomorrow night, you and me are watching some football. Be ready."

"Why don't we watch now?" Laney asked.

"I've got cross-country practice in half an hour. Mr. Beiderman is coming with me."

Mr. Beiderman was their third-floor neighbor and landlord. He had been a mysterious recluse until two years ago, when the Vanderbeekers had befriended him after he tried to kick them out of their apartment.

Jessie swallowed a bite of french toast, then looked at Orlando. "Tell me again why Mr. B joined your high school running team? He's like, old. As old as Papa."

"I can hear you," Papa called from the sink.

"He thought running with us would help him train for the marathon."

The New York City Marathon was like a citywide block party that happened the first Sunday of every November. It was for serious runners who raced to win money, but also for people who did it for fun. The Vanderbeekers loved watching the marathon every year and cheering on the runners. Because Harlem was located near the end of the course, many of the runners were exhausted by the time they ran past the Vanderbeekers and had leg cramps and needed encouragement.

Isa squinted. "Do you think Mr. Beiderman can run all 26.2 miles of the course? When he was training over the summer, he was sort of . . . well, you know . . ."

"Super out of shape?" Oliver offered from his spot at the stove.

"He was out of breath running around the playground with me," Laney reported. "I had to pat his back to help him breathe."

"How did he even qualify for the marathon? Don't you have to be a really good runner?" asked Jessie.

Orlando shrugged. "He's running with a charity. Anyway, he's not the worst runner on our cross-country team. That would be Stanley."

"Doesn't Stanley have asthma?" Jessie asked.

"He does," Orlando said. Finished with his french toast, he crunched into an apple he grabbed from the fruit bowl.

"Are *you* running the marathon?" Laney asked Orlando.

"Nope," he said. "You have to be at least eighteen years old."

"I still can't imagine Mr. Beiderman even *trying* a marathon," Jessie mused. "I mean, this is the guy who didn't leave his apartment for six years."

"I think he'll be okay," Orlando said. "I've been training with him a few mornings a week for a couple of months to help him get ready. On marathon day, my team will take turns running with him. Eight of us will be at different parts of the route, and we'll each run a couple of miles."

"Can *I* run with him?" Laney asked.

Orlando, done with his apple, started on a banana. "Nope. But when you're older you can."

Laney watched Orlando eat the banana in three bites. "I'm already six."

"We don't want you to be trampled," Isa told her. "Remember how many runners there are? Over fifty thousand. But don't forget that we're organizing the Halloween Five-K Fun Run at St. Nicholas Park. You can even run in your costume if you want."

"I can't wait for the fun run, but I'm going to run

the *real* New York City Marathon one day where all those people cheer for you and call out your name if you write it big on your shirt," Laney announced. "I'll start training right away." She pulled her turtleneck back up to her mouth, put her dishes in the dishwasher, and proceeded to run laps around the living room until she got so dizzy she fell down on the carpet and was rewarded by lots of dog kisses.

Two

After breakfast and cleanup, Orlando left for practice and the five Vanderbeeker kids walked down the street to the community garden on 141st Street, a space that used to be an empty lot filled with trash and weeds. A little over a year earlier, the Vanderbeekers had spent the summer cleaning it up and transforming it into a garden for Mr. Jeet and Miss Josie.

It was a perfect autumn day. The wind blew just enough to lightly rustle the leaves. The sky was a crystal-clear blue. They entered the garden, and Hyacinth led Franz and Billie Holiday to a patch of grass. Franz rolled over and relished a back rub against the stubby grass, his tail wagging at 150 wpm, or wags per minute. Billie Holiday, a primmer and more dignified dog, sat with her ears pricked forward and her nose at attention.

Miss Josie had asked Hyacinth to take Billie Holiday for the day because a hospital bed was being delivered for Mr. Jeet that morning. After a weeklong fundraiser in the neighborhood earlier that month, they had collected enough money for the bed rental. Not only would the hospital bed allow him to sit up with the press of a button, but the rails along its sides would keep him safe and give him something to hold on to when getting in and out of bed. Miss Josie had promised Laney that she could try it out later that afternoon.

The Vanderbeekers weren't the only ones in the garden. Next to them, Mr. Jones, the neighborhood mail carrier, carefully tended his plot, plucking dead leaves from his squash plants and pulling out flowers that had withered after a blast of cold weather. A few other neighbors were there as well, watering plants and cutting herbs to dry so they could use them through the winter. The sweet smell of sage drifted through the air.

Hyacinth sat on the grass with her newest knitting project while Laney rolled around on the grass with the dogs. Next to Hyacinth, Isa and Jessie both did their homework, their workload having increased considerably since they had started high school the previous month. Hyacinth peeked at Jessie's notebook. Her sister was writing down all sorts of numbers for her science experiment: the height of the plants, the number of leaves, the number of flowers, the time until blooming, and the branching of stems.

Hyacinth gazed at her family, their physical features a combination of their parents' ethnicities. Although Isa and Jessie were twins, Isa was rapidly growing to look more like their mom, with long, straight hair that fell over her shoulders like a waterfall, while Jessie looked a lot like Papa's side of the family, with hair that puffed out rather than flowing down. Oliver, who had always been skinny despite the many cookies he consumed every day, continued to grow taller without ever seeming to gain weight. Laney looked like an exact mix of her parents. It was as if a painter had blended her parents' skin tones to create one especially for her. As for Hyacinth, she thought she looked like Mama, but everyone said she had Papa's big smile.

"Hey, Vanderbeekers!"

The kids turned, and their friend Herman stepped into the garden with Purl One wrapped in her carrier. Hyacinth scrambled up to welcome him.

"How's Purl One?" she asked.

Herman leaned down, unsnapped the fabric around Purl One, and gently put her on the ground. The cat arched her back in a long stretch while Herman clipped a narrow leash to her harness.

Franz and Billie Holiday bounded over to greet Purl One. Franz licked her head, causing her hair to stick straight up as if she'd been electrocuted. Unbothered by her new hairstyle, Purl One crouched low to the ground and immediately pounced on a leaf that tumbled by.

"Did our mom give us cookies for the PM?" Hyacinth asked Herman.

He nodded and took off his backpack. "She gave us a dozen lemon drizzle cookies, and I brought some stuff from home." He unzipped his backpack and pulled out a bag of cookies, a quart of milk, an apple, and two cheese sticks.

"Nice," Hyacinth said. "Let's leave them in the shed."

Hyacinth took out of her backpack the scarf she had knit with thick black yarn. The evenings were chilly, and she was certain the PM could use a warm scarf.

"Want to bring the stuff into the shed with us?" Hyacinth asked Oliver. Hyacinth wasn't a huge fan of the shed. Over the summer, she had gone swimming at her friend's house, and they stored their inflatable toys in a shed very much like the one in this garden. Her friend had neglected to tell her that the shed was a favorite spot for wolf spiders, and when Hyacinth had gone in to retrieve a unicorn inner tube, an enormous wolf spider had jumped right on top of her head. Even though Mr. Beiderman, Papa, and Uncle Arthur had inspected the garden shed top to bottom multiple times and declared it wolf spider–free, Hyacinth still shuddered whenever she entered it.

When Oliver didn't look up from his book, Hyacinth sighed.

"Come on, Hyacinth," Herman said. "I'll protect you from the spiders."

Herman weaved through the garden plots and the lavender maze the Vanderbeekers had created in honor of Mr. Beiderman's daughter, who had passed away at age sixteen after being struck by a car. When he got to the shed, he opened the door, and Hyacinth peeked in. Everything looked the same as usual: the rakes and shovels were leaning against the corner, the buckets were nestled in a wobbly tower, and bags of soil were stacked neatly along the far wall.

Hyacinth worried about the person who was sleeping here. The shed was dark, and there were cracks in the wood-plank walls that let in the cold wind. The weather would only get worse as winter approached. What would the PM do then?

Herman entered the shed and placed the food parcels inside. Hyacinth took a deep breath and made her way to the spot where the PM had left a neat stack of clothes. She leaned over the soil stack to put the folded scarf on top of the PM's belongings. She wasn't trying to be nosy, she really wasn't, but the shirt on top, a gray one with white squares and green writing, seemed so familiar she had to look closer. She peered at the small writing, and for a second her heart stuttered.

"What?" Herman asked.

Hyacinth pointed to the shirt, and Herman stilled beside her. Hyacinth leaned down and picked it up. The T-shirt fluttered open, revealing a chart with white symbols and large green print along the top that read "I Wear This Shirt Periodically."

There were only two people in the entire neighborhood who had science-themed shirts like that. One was Jessie, and she definitely did *not* sleep in the shed at night.

Three

Jessie was trying to keep track of the number of leaves she had counted, which was more difficult than it sounds. She was concentrating so hard that she didn't notice how her siblings and Herman had gathered around her, blocking out the beam of sunshine that was helping her locate the smaller leaves.

"Can you guys move? I'm trying to record these findings . . ."

But there was a strange feeling in the air, something that made the little hairs on her arms prickle with unease. She looked up and noticed that Hyacinth was holding a gray T-shirt.

"What's wrong?" Jessie asked. The shirt was Orlando's, the one she had given him a couple of birthdays ago. She looked at Hyacinth. "How did you get that?"

"She found it in the shed," Isa said quietly.

Jessie's brow furrowed. "That's weird. Why would it be there?"

There was a long pause.

Jessie shook her head. "Wait. You think *Orlando* is the PM?"

Silence.

"That's ridiculous," Jessie said. "He probably just changed his shirt one day after working in the garden, then forgot it. Someone must have put it there for safekeeping."

Hyacinth and Herman glanced at each other, and Jessie glared back at them. "What?"

Hyacinth stared at the ground. "It was folded on top of the PM's clothes."

Jessie shook her head. She knew everything about Orlando; there was no way. "It couldn't possibly be him," she told them. "I mean, we would know if he lived in a *shed*, right? Anyway, we were just at his place!"

"That was a few months ago, before school ended," Oliver noted. "I remember, because it was right after my birthday."

Jessie remembered that too. It was the one time she had been to his apartment, and it hadn't even been an official invitation. Orlando had forgotten to bring Oliver's gift to his birthday party back in May, and he wanted to run into his apartment and pick it up. They'd been there only briefly—Orlando hadn't even invited them inside—and Jessie had caught a few glimpses of worn furniture and a stack of unwashed dishes by the sink.

Jessie glanced at her watch. It was almost noon; surely Orlando would be home from cross-country practice by now. She stood up and brushed her dirty hands against her pants. "Let's go over to his place and get this all cleared up."

Her siblings looked uneasily at her, but they followed her out of the garden. Herman, not wanting to keep Purl One out in the cold for long, headed uptown to the cat café and asked Hyacinth and Oliver to give him an update as soon as possible.

The walk down to 122nd Street was silent: an unusual state for the Vanderbeekers. The quiet gave Jessie time to think about the last few weeks. Had Orlando seemed different? She'd seen him doing laundry at Miss Josie's place the other day, but that wasn't unusual. His building didn't have a laundry room, so he often washed his clothes at the brownstone. He ate a ton of food whenever he was at their place—which was pretty much every day—but that wasn't unusual either. Mama always said teenage boys needed a lot of food. With each step toward his apartment, Jessie was more convinced that this whole idea was ridiculous.

But uneasy thoughts kept tumbling through her brain as she and her siblings turned east on Orlando's street and marched up to his building. A dumpster was parked in front; Franz barked at it and Billie Holiday eyed it warily. Jessie went to the entrance, located Orlando's apartment number on a silver panel to the right of the door, and pressed the buzzer for 2B.

She turned to her siblings when there was no answer. "He's probably in the shower." She buzzed again, but no one responded.

Orlando lived on the second floor, his windows facing the street. Jessie looked up, then toward her siblings, who were fanned out behind her.

"Hyacinth, if you get on my shoulders, you might be able to look into his window."

Hyacinth took a giant step backward, pulling Franz with her, and shook her head. "No, thank you."

"I'll do it!" Laney volunteered. She tried to pass Billie Holiday's leash to Isa, but her sister didn't take it.

"Laney, no," Isa said, turning to her twin sister. "Jess, this isn't a good idea."

"I just want to take a super-quick look inside," Jessie said. "Maybe he has music on and couldn't hear the doorbell ring."

Oliver glanced at the building. "You can scale it," he told her.

Jessie swiveled to look at her brother. "What?"

Oliver pointed to the concrete planter next to them. "Jump up on that," he said, pointing above them. "Put your hands on the windowsill, and use those two bricks jutting out for your feet. Then lift yourself up and you should be high enough to look through the window. I can do it if you want."

"No," Isa interjected again.

"I can do it," Jessie said.

"I don't think this is a good idea," Hyacinth said, covering her face with her hands.

"Me either," Isa said.

But Jessie didn't listen to her sisters' protests. She stepped up onto the planter, careful not to crush the bushes inside. She eased her way to the side of the building, standing on the tips of her sneakers to reach the windowsill.

"Now put your feet on those bricks," Oliver instructed.

Jessie moved one foot over, then the other. She slowly straightened her legs so she could see through the window.

"Almost there!" Oliver said.

"Be careful!" Hyacinth squeaked.

Jessie could almost see inside when an unfamiliar, authoritative voice rang out.

"Sure you want to do that?"

Jessie swung her head around and glimpsed a woman wearing a blue uniform and a shiny gold New York Police Department badge on her shirt. Then she lost her grip on the windowsill and fell backward into a cluster of bushes.

✴ ✴ ✴

"Jessie!" screeched Isa, Hyacinth, and Laney. Franz howled and Billie Holiday whimpered. They rushed to the bushes.

Oliver hung back. She hadn't fallen *that* far and was probably fine.

"You want to tell me what's going on?" the police officer asked Oliver. She peered at him over her sunglasses. The badge on her shirt said "Officer Ramos."

"Uh, our friend lives there?" Oliver said, pointing at the second-floor apartment.

"And you're trying to break in . . . why?" Officer Ramos asked him.

"We're not breaking in," Oliver explained. "We're trying to look through the window."

"Officer Ramos!"

Oliver glanced down the street. Another officer, this one holding two coffee cups and a brown bag under his arm, was speed walking toward them and saying "Ouch!" It looked as if hot coffee was splashing on his hands in his haste.

Officer Ramos sighed and muttered under her breath.

"You disappeared again," the other officer accused her. He was wearing a badge that said "Officer Pontas."

"I did *not* disappear," Officer Ramos told him. "I saw a disturbance, and I responded."

"*Without* your partner," Officer Pontas added.

"Look at these kids!" Officer Ramos said, gesturing to the Vanderbeekers. "They do not pose a severe security risk. I was assessing the situation." She pointed at Jessie, who was slowly climbing out of the bush she had fallen into. "Suspect A was attempting to enter that apartment."

"She was trying to see if her best friend was home," Oliver clarified. "He's gone missing."

Both officers went on high alert.

"How long has this person been missing?" they asked at the same time, whipping identical notebooks from their back pockets.

Oliver looked at the sky, thinking. "Like, two hours?"

The officers put their notebooks away.

"What is the missing person's name?" Officer Pontas asked, looking around as if searching for a more exciting and dangerous situation to address.

"Orlando Stewart," Oliver said.

Officer Ramos wrote the name down.

Oliver's sisters joined him. Jessie looked fine except for some leaves and twigs in her hair.

"I don't *think* Jessie needs to go to the hospital," Hyacinth reported to Oliver, "but her wrist looks swollen. Maybe we should get Dr. Rosengarten to check just in case."

"That's how my wrist always looks," Jessie told her.

"Who are you?" Laney asked the officers. "I'm Laney. I'm six years old, and this is Jessie, Isa, Hyacinth, Oliver, Franz, and Billie Holiday. Can you help us find our friend?"

"It sounds like your friend is fine if he's only been missing for a couple of hours," Officer Ramos said.

"I guess," Laney said, disappointed at their response.

The sound of static and a garbled voice came through Officer Pontas's walkie-talkie. He pulled it out of his pocket.

"Ooh, Oliver has a walkie-talkie too," Laney said, pointing.

"We've got to get going," Officer Pontas said to his partner, passing her a cup of coffee.

"Don't go sneaking into your friends' houses," Officer Ramos said to the kids, taking a big gulp of the coffee. " It's a crime punishable with eighteen years in prison." She took her cuffs out and swung them menacingly by her thumb and index finger.

Oliver's jaw dropped. "Seriously?"

"No," Officer Ramos said. "But don't do it again. It's creepy to look through people's windows."

The officers went down the street, and Isa glared at Jessie and Oliver.

"I told you not to do that," Isa said. "You could have been arrested."

"Should we wait for Orlando?" Oliver said. He sat down on the ledge of the large concrete planter and glanced down the street, looking for the familiar profile.

"I guess," Jessie said, sitting down next to him.

The Vanderbeekers sat there, watching people pass by. Laney took particular interest in a pair of chattering squirrels chasing each other from tree to tree. A cop car carrying Officer Ramos and Officer Pontas went past, and Laney waved at them. A teenager wearing sunglasses that covered nearly her whole face strolled by, bopping her head to the music on her headphones.

A few minutes later, the building door opened and two men wearing worn jeans and matching gray shirts that said "Mendoza Trash Removal" struggled to move a battered couch through the door. One of them was bald and wore glasses; the other had a faded gray baseball cap shoved on his head. Oliver got up to hold the door open for them. They nodded their thanks, then carried the couch out to the street and tossed it into the dumpster.

"Whoa," Laney said. "You're strong."

The guys nodded again. On the way back into the building, one of them propped open the door with a stopper. A few seconds later, they came down with a mattress. This time, Laney wasn't going to let them go by without finding out more. She jumped up and walked with them back to the building.

"What are you doing?" Laney asked.

"Emptying out an apartment," the guy with the cap said.

Laney's eyebrows creased in confusion. "Why?"

"Looks like the tenants got evicted. They left without taking their stuff," the guy with glasses added.

Oliver's breath caught in his throat. Surely they couldn't be talking about Orlando's place?

"Um, that apartment you're clearing? It's not 2B, is it?" Oliver asked.

The guys looked at each other.

"Yeah, I think it is," the guy in the cap said.

The Vanderbeekers raced toward the open building door.

"Hey!" one of the guys called out.

But they were already inside and running up the

stairs, Jessie leading the way and Franz howling right behind her. When Jessie got to the second floor, she stopped abruptly at the door to Orlando's apartment. Her siblings rammed into her, and Jessie threw her arms out, bracing herself against the door frame to keep from falling. They stared inside the apartment.

It was only until a man's voice saying "What are you doing here?" that they turned around to find a person wearing a dark-green work shirt with the word "Superintendent" stitched above the left pocket.

"This is private property," the super said, his face red and sweaty and mad.

"Our friend lives here," Oliver explained, "and those guys are throwing away his stuff!"

"The Stewarts don't live here anymore, if that's who you're looking for," the man said.

"Wait, what?" Jessie said. "What happened?"

"I evicted them," the man said. "They hadn't paid their rent in three months. When they finally left, I had to pay for a dumpster because they left all their stuff. They're not getting their security deposit back, that's for sure."

"So you just . . . kicked them out of their home?" Hyacinth asked.

"If you don't pay, you don't stay," the man said with a shrug. "Now you kids need to leave the building. This is called trespassing."

Oliver looked into the apartment. There was a stack of Orlando's science books. Two football jerseys lay on the ground. In the corner was a small bear wearing a T-shirt with the Franklin Institute logo on it that Laney had bought for him over the summer when the Vanderbeekers visited the science museum in Philadelphia.

"Please," Jessie said, her eyes wide and panicked. "At least let us grab some of their things. He's our friend."

The super looked unconvinced and annoyed, then Isa spoke up in a low, quiet voice.

"You're just going to throw it away," Isa said reasonably. "Give us five minutes, then you'll never see us again."

The super glanced at his watch. "Five minutes. That's it."

The Vanderbeekers ran inside. Jessie passed out a handful of shopping bags that she found under the kitchen sink. Laney ran for the bear and put it in her bag while Isa and Jessie went for the books. Oliver grabbed the football jerseys, and Hyacinth went through his dresser and grabbed clothes until her bag was overflowing.

"Time's up," the super said. The two guys doing the trash removal were behind him, looking sympathetic but also ready to finish their job.

Isa thanked the super (which Oliver thought was completely unnecessary), and the Vanderbeekers took their bags downstairs and out the door. They stood in front of the building wondering what to do next.

"We need to find him," Jessie said, and her siblings agreed. They dragged the bags to Marcus Garvey Park a few blocks away, where the team often ran along the park's walking paths. Orlando was nowhere to be seen. Jessie pulled out her phone and called him, but the phone just rang and rang. She was about to dial his number again when Isa gently took the phone away and put it in her own pocket.

"Where is he?" Jessie said, letting the bag of books

fall to the ground. She crossed her arms on her chest and crouched on the sidewalk, hunching her shoulders as if protecting her heart from breaking.

"We're going to find him," Isa said, putting her arm around Jessie's shoulders. "He's going to be okay."

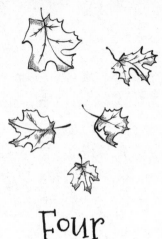

Four

The Vanderbeekers headed back uptown, jumping on the subway because of the bags. Instead of going home, they made their way to the Treehouse Bakery and Cat Café.

Isa immediately felt her body relax when she spotted the cat café. It was like a beacon on 143rd Street. Delicate lace curtains allowed a glimpse into the cozy space through the large french windows, and mums in burgundy, sunshine yellow, and burnt orange were settled into window boxes. A large orange-and-white cat sat on the windowsill, observing their approach with focused, unblinking eyes.

Isa helped Hyacinth tie Billie Holiday and Franz to a pipe in front of the bakery where there was a bowl of water for animals passing by. Then she opened the door and the Vanderbeekers squeezed through the entrance with all of the bags. Purl One immediately greeted them and pounced on their sneakers, gripping Oliver's shoelaces in her mouth and giving them a strong yank. Oliver leaned down and carefully disentangled the laces from her teeth, then picked her up and settled her inside the front of his hoodie as if she were a kangaroo baby. Mama, who was unloading a tray of cookies into the display counter, looked up.

"Hey," she said. "What's with all the bags?"

"We need to talk to you about something," Isa said.

Mama's brow creased in worry. "Uh-oh. What did you do now?"

"Nothing bad," Oliver said hurriedly, but Mama's forehead refused to smooth out.

"Take the table by the window so you can keep an eye on Billie Holiday and Franz," Mama said. "I'll be right there."

Isa shoved the bags of Orlando's belongings under the table, and the Vanderbeekers took seats and waited for Mama. Hyacinth picked up one of the adoptable kittens and brushed her fingers against its forehead.

Laney pulled her turtleneck to her mouth and chewed on the fold. Oliver, who still had Purl One in his hoodie, traced his fingertips along the grooves in the wood table. Jessie sat hunched in her chair, staring out the window, one foot tapping an erratic beat against the ground.

Mama arrived with a tray of teacups and a teapot that released a trail of fragrant steam from its spout. She also set down a plate piled with cookies and fruit, but no one had an appetite, not even Oliver.

"Talk to me," Mama said, settling herself between Jessie and Isa.

Jessie was a statue, not taking her eyes from the window.

Isa looked at her siblings, then back at their mom. "You know how we've been leaving food for the Person of Mystery?"

Mama's stranger-danger radar went on alert. "Did you see this person? Is everything okay?"

"We didn't see the PM, but we have a good idea who he is," Oliver said. "Hyacinth found this in the shed." He slid the T-shirt across the table to Mama.

Mama's hand flew to her mouth. "But . . . how could . . . That's Orlando's . . ."

"We went to his apartment," Isa continued, "and two men were emptying it out. Just tossing his stuff into a dumpster. The super said the Stewarts haven't paid the rent in three months, so the management company evicted them two weeks ago. He gave us five minutes to grab some of Orlando's things." She gestured to the bags surrounding them.

"We tried looking for him at cross-country practice, but he wasn't there. His phone just rang and rang," Hyacinth said.

"What should we do?" Isa finished.

Mama's eyes were bright, as if she were trying to blink back an emotion that she didn't want her kids to see. "I think," she said, "we need to talk to Miss Josie."

☼ ☼ ☼

Mama took the rest of the day off work, instructing the store manager to close early if they ran out of cookies. The Vanderbeekers headed for home, the two dogs leading the way. Autumn was showing its colors, the leaves on the trees a mix of reds, oranges, and golds. The brownstones and buildings along their path were adorned with pumpkins and Halloween decorations: cotton stretched thin to look like cobwebs; black plastic spiders the size of quarters perched on fences; and, at one building, a set of fake gravestones that Hyacinth refused to look at.

On 141st Street, the Vanderbeekers navigated the slightly uneven sidewalks where tree roots had pushed up the concrete. They had memorized every bump and crack many years ago. The trees, growing in pits spaced about twenty feet apart and surrounded by foot-tall fence guards, stretched their limbs toward the sky, competing for sunshine with the buildings that surrounded them. Laney brushed her hands against the tree trunks as she passed, running her fingers against the rough bark and trying to absorb comfort from the old maple trees.

As Laney walked down the block, she chewed on her turtleneck and thought about Orlando. She knew some homeless people in her neighborhood. There was Osbourne, who spent his days on the corner of 137th Street and Frederick Douglass Boulevard and held open doors at Uptown Grocer in hopes of tips. He spent his nights at a men's shelter in East Harlem and went to local churches during the day for meals and showers. Laney also knew of a man who sometimes sat in a wheelchair by the subway turnstiles at 135th Street. He sort of scared her because his eyes were always closed and he moaned as if in pain. Sometimes she left a snack from her backpack next to his wheelchair, but she never knew if he found it.

Laney had never thought about *kids* not having a place to live—or having to sleep in a tiny, dark shed. It made her stomach feel hollow and empty.

When they arrived at the brownstone, they dropped off Franz and left Orlando's things in the basement. Then they all went up to the second floor with Billie Holiday. Oliver knocked on the door, and a few seconds later Miss Josie appeared and Billie Holiday wiggled her way into the apartment and beelined for Mr. Jeet.

"Hello, my dears!" Miss Josie said, her face filled with a beautiful smile. "Come see the hospital bed!" Her smile vanished at the sight of their somber faces.

"Is everything okay?" she asked.

Mama ushered the kids into the apartment. The hospital bed was set up in the living room, right next to a window. Mr. Jeet was sitting in his wheelchair next to the couch, and his eyes sparkled when he saw them. Laney ran to him and wrapped her arms around his neck and kissed his cheek. Then she reached her hand into her pocket and pulled out a rock she had collected and put it into Mr. Jeet's hand.

"Why is the hospital bed in the living room?" Laney asked, pointing.

"It was too wide to fit through our bedroom door," Miss Josie explained. "But I think it works fine to have it in the living room. Why don't you try it out?"

Laney nodded, then crawled up onto the bed and rolled around, bumping into the safety bars on each side. "It's so comfortable!" she announced.

"Don't give her the remote," Oliver said, but it was too late. Laney had already located it hanging on the rail and was making the back of the bed lower and rise.

Mama took a seat on the couch next to Mr. Jeet in his wheelchair, and Isa and Jessie settled down next to her. Hyacinth stood next to Mr. Jeet, gripping his hand, and Oliver paced restlessly around the living room. Laney was still playing with the hospital bed.

"You guys are making me worried," Miss Josie said.

"The kids," Mama began, "have found some things in the garden shed that might reveal who has been sleeping there."

"Oh gracious," Miss Josie said, turning her head to look at Mr. Jeet before her eyes met Mama's again. "Is it someone we know?"

Mr. Jeet made a noise and his right arm reached forward. Oliver hurried over and grabbed him in case he lost his balance and tipped out of the wheelchair.

"Yes," Mama said. "It's someone you know."

Five

Miss Josie fingered the T-shirt that Jessie had given her. "He promised he would tell me if this happened again."

"What do you mean, *again*?" Jessie asked, squinting.

Miss Josie sighed. "Remember when he spent the summer here, a few years ago?"

The Vanderbeekers nodded.

"It was the same situation, only back then he called us when his mom didn't come home for two nights. We took the next flight to Georgia, picked him up, and brought him back here. We finally heard from his mom a few weeks later, and together we decided to keep Orlando for the rest of the summer while his mom worked out whatever was going on. At the end of August, we took him back to Georgia and made sure his mom was doing okay before leaving him there. We wanted to be his guardians, but she didn't want that."

"What does that mean?" Laney asked. "Being his guardians?"

"It would mean we would take care of him permanently, as if we were his parents," Miss Josie said. "We wanted that very much."

"He never said anything about his mom disappearing," Jessie said, her face stricken. "I had no idea."

"He didn't want to talk about it," Miss Josie explained. "It was a really confusing time for him."

"What do you think we should do?" Mama asked. Her hands were pressed before her face in a prayer.

"Let me get the full story first," Miss Josie said. "I'll call around to my folks in Georgia and try to reach Orlando's mom. Then we need to talk to Orlando tonight."

The Vanderbeekers gave Miss Josie some privacy while she got on the phone, calling family back in Georgia to ask if they had heard anything from Orlando's mom in the last month. Miss Josie asked the Vanderbeekers to come up to their apartment that night for dinner. As always, Orlando was planning on eating at the brownstone.

The Vanderbeekers went back down to their apartment, and the afternoon dragged on. Jessie and Isa made their way to the basement, taking refuge next to the whistling radiator and burrowing into the nest they created with the throw pillows. When Isa eventually got up to practice her violin, Jessie tortured herself by looking up *homelessness* on her phone. There were so many statistics: one study said that 4.2 million kids experience homelessness in America each year. She read about how in New York City, one in ten kids was sleeping in a homeless shelter or in the home of friends or relatives. As she read, she wondered if there were people in her own class and school who lived in shelters.

After an hour, she felt Isa's hand on her shoulder.

"Hey," Isa said. "Why don't you take a break from the research? Maybe we're making assumptions and there's an explanation for all of this. Orlando's mom could have found another place in the area. Remember how Orlando's always complaining about how mean their building manager is? He talked about the possibility of moving a few months ago."

Jessie put down her phone. "Yeah," she said, trying to breathe through her worry. "Maybe everything is okay."

They headed upstairs, where Mama was making dinner: cauliflower Parmesan and a gigantic salad. Hyacinth was sitting on the floor leaning against the couch, knitting with a vengeance, Franz's head on her lap and one of his ears flipped open to the ceiling. Oliver was sprawled on the couch reading *Other Words for Home* by Jasmine Warga.

"What's with the super-speedy knitting?" Jessie asked, pushing Oliver's legs off the couch so she could sit down.

"She's stress knitting," Oliver commented from behind his book. "She thinks she needs to make Orlando enough cold-weather accessories to last him until he's eighty."

Hyacinth's brow furrowed. "I just want him to be warm. Being cold is the worst." She continued to knit, the ends of her needles bouncing against Franz's head as she worked.

Isa sat on the carpet next to Laney, who had spread out her whole shell collection from the beach over the summer. She was carefully pasting googly eyes on them.

"Hey, Laney," Isa said as she watched Laney arrange and rearrange the shells. "At dinner, don't mention anything about the shed or the apartment we went to see today, or about our conversation with Miss Josie. Okay?"

"You know what, Laney?" Oliver piped in. "Maybe don't even talk to Orlando. Or look at him."

Laney turned to face Oliver, her hands on her hips. "I can talk to Orlando if I want to."

Isa walked over and put her arm over Laney's shoulders. "What Oliver means," she said, narrowing her eyes at her brother, "is that we should let Miss Josie do the talking. Orlando might be sensitive about what's going on, and we should see how he feels instead of bombarding him with questions and worries."

"I have a *lot* of questions for him," Jessie said, glowering from the couch and ignoring Hyacinth. "Number one: What the heck is going on? Number two: Why did you hide this huge thing from your best friend?"

Isa sighed and got ready to launch into her let's-not-jump-to-conclusions speech again, when the doorbell rang.

"He's here! He's here!" Laney shrieked, running toward the door, Franz and Tuxedo racing after her.

"Just act normal, just act normal," Hyacinth whispered to herself, her knitting needles clacking furiously.

Laney flung open the door. "Orlando!" she said, wrapping her arms around him so suddenly that he had to helicopter his arms to keep his balance. "You're okay!"

"Wow," Orlando said. "That's a . . . strange welcome. Why wouldn't I be okay?"

"She's been like this all day," Isa interjected. "Don't mind her."

Orlando, finally released from Laney's grip, paused as he took off his coat, and looked in surprise at the five Vanderbeeker kids lined up in front of him. "What's going on?"

Laney gripped the top of her turtleneck with both hands and pulled it so high that it covered her mouth and rested right under her nose.

"Nothing!" Isa said. "Everything's fine!"

"Where have you been?" Jessie asked, crossing her arms and glowering at Orlando. "I've been calling nonstop."

"I didn't have my phone with me today," Orlando said. "Did you need something?"

"You would know if you picked up your phone. And when I called, it didn't go to voicemail or anything," Jessie pressed. "It just rang and rang."

"That's weird," Orlando said, turning away to hang up his coat.

"*It's weird?*" Jessie said, her voice rising. "Or maybe it's because—"

"Orlando!" Mama interrupted Jessie, coming in from the kitchen. "How are you, honey? I made your favorite dinner tonight, cauliflower Parmesan with garlic bread and Caesar salad."

"Wow, Mrs. Vanderbeeker, that's so nice of you—"

"And for dessert, pound cake with raspberry drizzle!" she finished.

"Pound cake!" Laney said from behind her turtle-neck. "I love pound cake!"

Orlando's smile dimmed. "Mrs. Vanderbeeker," he said, his eyes creased in puzzlement, "you know my birthday isn't until February."

"I was in the mood to cook. We're eating at your aunt and uncle's place tonight. Help me bring the food upstairs, okay?"

The Vanderbeekers and Orlando grabbed the dishes from the kitchen and made their way to Miss Josie and Mr. Jeet's apartment on the second floor. Miss Josie had the door open before they knocked.

"Hello!" she said, her eyes seeking out Orlando. Even though there was a big smile on her face, her eyes were worried.

"Hey, Aunt Josie," Orlando said, leaning down to kiss her cheek.

She patted his shoulder, then turned away. "Come in, come in."

Jessie noticed that Miss Josie wiped her eyes as she led them into the kitchen.

"Mrs. Vanderbeeker made a feast," Orlando commented as he laid the huge baking dish of cauliflower

Parmesan on the counter and took off the flowered oven mitts he had been wearing. He turned to face the living room and spotted the hospital bed.

"Hey! The bed looks great!" Orlando said. "But why's it in the living room?"

"Didn't fit through the bedroom door," Laney said with authority. "Want to try it? I'll show you."

Orlando laughed. "I'd probably break it!"

She eyed his football-player frame, then shook her head. "It would be fine for you. I bounced on it and everything."

Another knock on the door revealed Mr. Beiderman in his signature all-black outfit with his cat, Princess Cutie, in his arms. Mr. Beiderman's eyes settled for a moment on Orlando before scanning the rest of the room. "Hi," he said gruffly.

Laney ran to him and gave him a hug, and Princess Cutie hopped into Laney's embrace.

"Come, come," Miss Josie said. "Let's eat before the food gets cold."

Miss Josie and Mr. Jeet had only a small dining table that could seat four at a squeeze, so people filled up their dishes at the kitchen counter and then found seats in the living room. Miss Josie made a plate for Mr. Jeet and brought it to him, pulling out a side table that swung right in front of his wheelchair so he could eat comfortably. Laney wanted to sit next to him on the couch, but Papa steered her toward the table. She'd been forbidden to eat on Miss Josie's pristine couch ever since she'd upended a bowl of tomato soup on it the previous month.

Once everyone was settled, Mama gave thanks for the food and they dug in. Jessie sat next to Orlando on the long couch, seemingly one hundred percent focused on her food, while Isa sat on his other side and kept up a stream of chatter to fill the uncomfortable silence. She talked about the violin piece she was working on and about the annoying kid in her chamber group who never practiced, and about her teacher, Mr. Van Hooten, who had recently adopted his first pet, an enormous gray cat he had fallen in love with at the Treehouse Bakery and Cat Café. He had named the cat Arpeggio, and his love for it was beginning to rival his love for the violin.

Hyacinth looked forlornly at Orlando between bites of her garlic bread (she refused to touch the cauliflower Parmesan; cauliflower was ghost broccoli), and Oliver kept tapping his foot nervously on the floor. Mama, Papa, Mr. Beiderman, and Miss Josie were having a hushed conversation near the kitchen, stopping suddenly whenever any of the kids glanced at them.

After dinner, Mama served slices of pound cake with generous spoonfuls of raspberry compote and a swirl of whipped cream. Then Miss Josie took Isa's seat on the couch so she could be next to Orlando. Everyone gathered around, waiting and watching. Orlando, realizing that all eyes were on him, froze mid-chew.

Miss Josie put her hand on Orlando's. "Orlando, how are things going with you?"

Orlando swallowed, then coughed. Isa passed him her glass of water.

He took a sip. "Things are fine." Nine pairs of eyes looked at him. "Um, how are all of you doing? Am I missing something? I feel like I'm missing something."

"I just want to make sure everything is okay," Miss Josie said. "I haven't heard from your mom lately."

Orlando's face went carefully blank. "She's fine."

"Really?" Miss Josie asked.

"Yep," Orlando said, staring down at his dessert plate.

"What's she doing tonight?" Miss Josie probed.

There was a long silence. The brownstone itself seemed to still, as if holding its breath.

Finally, Jessie couldn't hold it in anymore. She jumped to her feet. "Stop lying to us!" she bit out, her voice ringing throughout the room, her hands jammed on her hips. "Tell us the *truth*."

A long silence followed, everyone frozen in the moment.

"You found out," Orlando said at last, his voice quiet, his shoulders hunched in surrender.

Jessie deflated. "Then it's true. You're the one who's been sleeping in the garden shed."

Orlando looked up, then nodded. "Yes."

"Orlando, honey, why didn't you say anything?" Miss Josie said, tears springing into her eyes. "Why didn't you come to us?"

"I thought she was coming back," Orlando said, his eyes pleading. "She sometimes disappears for a few days, but this time she didn't come back for a week. I kept calling, but she never picked up the phone. Please don't call the police on her."

Miss Josie stilled. "Oh, Orlando, I don't want her to get in trouble either, but she abandoned you and left you without a place to live. When I think about you living in that shed, all alone . . ."

"Wait, your mom just disappears?" Laney said. She looked at Mama in panic.

"I promise I won't," Mama said, blinking rapidly.

"It's fine," Orlando said. "She's done this before. I thought she would come back, but then Mr. Carvel started asking about the rent. When I got the eviction notice, I had no choice. I had to leave."

"I thought it was only that one time . . . when you stayed with us that summer. Has it happened more than that?" Miss Josie asked, her face stricken.

Orlando shifted in his seat. "There might have been a few more times back in Georgia. But it wasn't very long, and I stayed with Aunt Tammy."

"Wait, isn't Aunt Tammy the one who smells like boiled cabbage and complains about you eating too much?" Jessie asked.

Orlando shrugged. "She's not that bad."

"I don't understand why you didn't come to us," Miss Josie told him. "We were right here. We could have helped. To think you've been living in the shed . . ."

"You've had so much going on," Orlando said, his eyes darting to Mr. Jeet. "I didn't want to make a big deal about it. I thought my mom was coming back, and I didn't want to inconvenience you . . ."

"You are *not* an inconvenience, and you are *not* going back to that shed. You're living with us now."

"I couldn't do that, Aunt Josie," he said. "There's more space for me in Georgia. I can always stay with Aunt Tammy again. My mom will probably end up back there anyway. She never liked the city."

"You *can't* move to Georgia," Laney said. "We need you here!"

"You're not going," Oliver said flatly. "We won't let you."

Orlando looked at Miss Josie. "I can't stay here. This place is too small for another person."

"Nonsense," Miss Josie said, waving a hand. "I've

already fixed up our bedroom for you. I was planning on sleeping in the living room anyway, since the hospital bed is here. The bedroom is empty."

"But, Aunt Josie—"

"Who's going to help me train for the marathon if you leave?" Mr. Beiderman demanded.

"The other guys can—" Orlando began.

"What about this year's science fair plans?" Jessie asked. "We've got to keep our winning streak going."

"*You're* the science genius," Orlando said. "You don't need me."

"Don't you *want* to stay here?" Laney interjected.

Orlando hesitated. "I do, but—"

Miss Josie grabbed his hand. "Stay until the marathon. That's only two weeks away. Take some time to think about what you want, and meanwhile, we'll keep looking for your mom. If it doesn't work out for you to stay here, we'll find another solution. And if you want to go back to Georgia in two weeks, we'll make the arrangements."

"Aunt Josie . . ." Orlando began again.

"Don't you even think about arguing with me right now, Orlando," Miss Josie said, her eyebrows set in a firm line. "Mr. Jeet and I love you more than the moon and the stars. We are family, and this is how we are handling the situation right now." Her voice broke.

"Yes, ma'am," Orlando replied.

And the Vanderbeekers, Miss Josie and Mr. Jeet, and Mr. Beiderman—all the people who loved him—watched as Orlando quietly excused himself and went into Miss Josie and Mr. Jeet's bedroom, now his own temporary bedroom, and closed the door.

Six

Later, back in their apartment, Isa reflected that in all the years she had known Orlando, she had never met his mom. When he'd lived with Mr. Jeet and Miss Josie four summers ago, he'd come alone on a plane while his mom had stayed in Georgia. And since he had moved to Harlem, his mother hadn't once come to their Mega Family Dinners, when everyone who lived in the brownstone joined them. Isa had asked Orlando about it, but he always had an excuse for his mom: she was busy at work, she was out with friends, she didn't feel well. This, Isa now realized, should have raised alarm bells. Most of her friends mentioned their parents at least once in a while. Her friend Allegra loved to complain about her workaholic parents, who were both pediatricians, but Isa knew that they were around — she saw them when she dropped by Allegra's house.

Orlando, on the other hand, had always been mysterious about his family. Isa wondered if he talked to Jessie about it.

"Hey," Isa said, grabbing Jessie's hand and pulling her to her feet. "Let's go pick up Orlando's things from the garden."

Jessie let herself be dragged out of the brownstone, and the twins walked to the garden in silence. After entering the gates, they made their way through the winding vines and plants toward the back fence. The sun was setting, and a dusky quiet had descended.

Jessie paused when she opened the door to the shed. It was dark and cold inside. She stood there, staring into the tiny, damp space.

Isa looked over Jessie's shoulder into the inky darkness. How could Orlando sleep there? It was seriously creepy. Isa didn't even like going in there to grab gardening equipment; she always made Jessie or Oliver do it.

Jessie stepped all the way in and sank onto a bag of soil.

"I can't believe he's been living in here," she said. "Why didn't he ask for help? We would have helped him!"

Isa sat down next to Jessie and put an arm around her shoulders. "Maybe he felt ashamed? Or he hoped his mom would come back?"

Jessie's hands clenched into fists. "I'm his best friend. Shouldn't he tell me things? Isn't that what friends do? Shouldn't I have known that they got evicted? And that he was living in a freaking *shed*?"

And for the first time in many years, Jessie began to cry.

✦　✦　✦

Jessie had kept it together all day. She had kept it together when she went to Orlando's apartment building and learned about him and his mom being evicted. She'd made it through that very painful dinner, and she'd even kept her cool when Orlando confessed to sleeping in the shed. But now, sitting in the darkness, feeling the cold wind blow through the slats of the shed walls, she couldn't hold it in any longer. The sobs burst from her chest as if she would explode if they didn't come out. She felt Isa holding her tight, trying to keep her from floating off into that place where grief goes.

Just when she thought she had a handle on herself, she imagined Orlando packing his stuff up and closing the door to his apartment for the last time. Orlando opening the shed and trying to find a comfortable place to sleep. Orlando thinking there was no option but to figure it out on his own.

Finally, Jessie felt as if she had cried every last tear out of her body. Isa continued to rub her back as Jessie took one final swipe at her eyes. "I'm okay," she told Isa. "Thanks."

"We'll get through this," Isa told her.

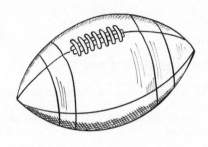

Seven

Hyacinth, Oliver, and Laney stood in front of the living room window, waiting for Isa and Jessie to return from the garden with Orlando's things. Mama and Papa were up in their room, speaking in such hushed whispers that none of the kids could tell what they were saying, even when their ears were pressed against the door.

It was eight thirty, and the sun had set an hour earlier. Laney was supposed to be getting ready for bed. Franz perched his front feet on the windowsill, howling whenever a dog or a bike passed by. Tuxedo paced back and forth, hiding herself behind the curtains and occasionally popping out to surprise Franz. George

Washington watched from the other armchair, his eyes half-shut and his tail flicking lazily.

"Do you think Orlando will go back to Georgia?" Hyacinth asked.

Laney took a break from chewing on the neck of her shirt. "Of course not. He can't leave us. We need him."

"That's not how it works," Oliver said. "I mean, he always talks about how pretty Georgia is. It doesn't get super cold in the winter like it does here, and you know how he hates being cold. Plus he misses football."

Laney shrugged. "He does lots of sports here. He's really good at running."

Oliver shook his head. "Running isn't the same. Football is in his *blood*."

"Eww!" Laney said, scrunching her nose. "His blood? Yuck!"

"Football is dangerous," Hyacinth reported. "Like, he could die from getting hit in the head. That's why he needs to stay here with us. He can be a professional runner instead."

Oliver's eyes lit up. "You know what? There's a prize for winning the marathon. Maybe Orlando can win the marathon and get rich, and then he could get his own apartment and he wouldn't have to worry about money."

"Ooh, good idea!" Laney said, her eyes brightening.

"You can't run in the marathon until you're eighteen," Hyacinth said. "Remember?"

"But Mr. Beiderman is running it!" Laney said. "Maybe *he* can win the marathon and give the money to Orlando." She beamed, confident that the problem had been solved.

Oliver rolled his eyes. "The chances of Mr. Beiderman winning the marathon are zero in a billion."

"Papa says we can do anything if we put our minds to it," Laney said. "I *believe* Mr. Beiderman can win!"

Oliver banged his forehead against the window a few times. "Where are they?" he grumbled.

"I see them!" Laney yelled as her sisters' familiar silhouettes appeared under a streetlamp.

The three Vanderbeeker kids, plus Franz and Tuxedo, raced to the door and threw it open.

"Yikes! What happened to your face?" Oliver asked Jessie.

"Nothing! Geez," Jessie said, rubbing her eyes and turning away from her younger siblings.

"It looks like you had an allergic reaction," Oliver continued. "Your eyes are all puffy."

Isa jabbed her elbow into his side. "Seriously, Oliver, stop it."

"We've been waiting and waiting for you," Laney said. "I'm supposed to be getting ready for bed, but I'm not tired at all."

"I need to be by myself," Jessie mumbled as she headed up the stairs.

"By yourself?" Laney exclaimed. "Really?"

Jessie didn't turn back.

"She needs some space," Isa said to Laney, resting a hand on her shoulder.

They heard Jessie's footsteps heading to the bedroom, followed by the familiar screech of a window sliding open.

"She's going to the REP," Oliver noted.

The REP, or Roof of Epic Proportions, was at the top of the brownstone and was accessible by the fire-escape stairs outside Jessie and Isa's bedroom, as well as by a hatch on the third floor in front of Mr. Beiderman's apartment.

"It's a good place to think," Hyacinth said, nodding.

"I want to go up there too," Laney said, tugging at Isa's hand.

Isa pulled her into a hug, and Laney sank into her sister's embrace.

"Why do bad things happen to good people?" Laney asked.

Isa rocked her back and forth. "I don't know. It doesn't seem right, does it?"

✦ ✦ ✦

Jessie climbed up the fire escape, her footsteps light as she made her way to the roof. One floor up, she passed Miss Josie and Mr. Jeet's apartment. The bedroom window was cracked open, but the shades were drawn. Jessie planned to keep going up, but the sound of Miss Josie's voice stopped her.

"I just got a phone call from your mom," Miss Josie said.

"Is she okay?" Orlando asked. "Can I talk to her?"

Jessie inched closer to the window so she could hear better.

"She called from a pay phone," Miss Josie said. "Our conversation was so brief, I didn't have a chance to ask her anything before she hung up."

"She didn't want to talk to me?" Orlando asked.

"She said she tried to call you but the call didn't go through."

"My phone stopped working last week," Orlando said. "I guess she didn't pay the bill."

"Oh, honey," Miss Jeet said. "We'll get that connected again right away. I'm sure she'll call soon."

There was a long silence, then Orlando's voice: "Where was she?"

"She's on her way to Georgia. She wants you to go down there and stay with Aunt Tammy again, and she'll get you when she has a job and an apartment."

Another long silence.

"Unless . . ." Miss Josie began.

"Unless what?" Orlando asked, his voice rough and tired.

"Unless you want to stay here. With us. Permanently."

"I couldn't do that," Orlando said. "I already feel awful about taking your bedroom."

"We would love it if you stayed. We could apply for guardianship," Miss Josie said.

"Can I think about it?" Orlando asked.

"Of course," Miss Josie said, "but I want you to stay here at least until the marathon while we work on some options for you."

The light flicked off, and the bedroom went dark. Jessie leaned closer, wanting to knock on the glass, but she changed her mind and silently went up the fire escape, her mind filled with all she had just heard.

✿ ✿ ✿

"It's time for a family meeting," Hyacinth said to Laney and Isa as she brushed Franz's fur.

"Did someone say 'family meeting'?" Oliver asked, popping his head into Hyacinth and Laney's room.

"Why do we need a family meeting?" Isa asked as she tidied up her sisters' room. She grabbed discarded clothes and threw them into the hamper, gathered

Franz's dog toys and tossed them into a basket, and placed books back on the shelves.

Laney rolled her eyes. "Because of *Orlando.*"

Isa shook her head. "I don't think we should get involved."

Oliver, Hyacinth, and Laney were aghast.

"Why not?" Laney asked.

"We *always* get involved. Always!" Hyacinth exclaimed.

"Has Jessie had enough alone time yet?" Laney asked, looking at her wrist even though she had never worn a watch in her life. "Let's go up to the REP."

Isa shook her head. "It's time for bed."

"Please?" Laney asked. "Pleasepleaseplease?"

Isa sighed. "Okay, but only for a few minutes."

The Vanderbeekers went to the twins' bedroom and raided the closet for cozy hoodies. Laney put on her favorite, Isa's dark-green summer camp sweatshirt. It went down to her knees, and she had to roll up the sleeves five times before her hands showed.

The window was already open from Jessie's exit, so the Vanderbeekers piled onto the fire escape and started ascending the creaky metal stairs. They passed Mr.

Jeet and Miss Josie's living room window. Mr. Jeet lay in his new hospital bed, the back raised so he could watch the news. Miss Josie was sitting next to him, knitting. She waved as she saw the kids go up. The fire escape also passed by the second-floor bedroom, but it was dark and the shades were drawn.

They continued their journey up and went by Mr. Beiderman's apartment. Mr. Beiderman was nowhere to be seen, but Princess Cutie was perched in the windowsill, and she batted the window as they passed.

"She's giving us high fives!" Laney squealed, putting her palm on the window to return the gesture.

Usually Mr. Beiderman liked to work after dinner. He used his small second bedroom as an office, and it was there that he did his mysterious art history stuff. None of the Vanderbeekers quite knew what his work consisted of. Sometimes he went to conferences, and other times they saw him lugging heavy books up to his apartment. Once Orlando had asked him about a project he was working on, and Mr. Beiderman spoke about expanding or potentially deconstructing the art history canon. Laney had been instantly confused; it sounded as if Mr. Beiderman was talking about shooting cannons at paintings. When he had finally stopped half an hour later, the Vanderbeekers were politely nodding even though they had no idea what he had been saying. Orlando, however, had nodded in agreement, as if the deconstruction of the art history canon made complete sense to him.

Laney was the first to reach the roof. She saw Jessie sitting in one of the Adirondack chairs that Oliver and Hyacinth had made with Uncle Arthur over the summer. Oliver and Hyacinth had had the idea of converting the roof to something more than a boring building rooftop. After several ideas, including a swimming pool, a dance party space, and a ball pit, they decided to create their own personal rooftop theater. With so many Vanderbeekers, going out to watch a movie in the theater was a rare occurrence. Movie tickets in New York City were expensive; for the whole family to go, it could cost almost a hundred and twenty dollars. And that was without popcorn.

With Uncle Arthur, Hyacinth and Oliver had designed a frame onto which they could slide a white bedsheet Hyacinth had sewn together like a giant pillowcase; that served as the screen. Then they had constructed ten Adirondack chairs. Hyacinth had painted them the colors of the rainbow. Now, whenever they wanted to watch a movie, Papa would borrow the projector from his job doing computer repair work and connect it to his laptop. Then Mama would make their favorite popcorn flavors: sea salt caramel, Parmesan herb, and white chocolate and cherry. The only unfortunate thing about the rooftop theater was not being able to go up there in bad weather.

Tonight, however, the Vanderbeekers weren't on the roof to see a movie. They had business to take care of.

"What are you doing up here?" Jessie said when she saw her siblings.

"Family meeting," Hyacinth announced.

Jessie nodded, then leaned forward and rested her elbows on her knees. "I overheard Orlando and Miss Josie talking when I was coming up here. His mom contacted Miss Josie, and she wants Orlando to go back to Georgia and stay with his Aunt Tammy until she's ready to take care of him again."

"What?" exclaimed Isa, Oliver, Hyacinth, and Laney.

"Yes," Jessie said. "But Miss Josie said she and Mr. Jeet want to be his guardians."

"He's staying!" Laney said, jumping up and down.

"Shh!" Isa and Jessie said.

"That would be perfect," Oliver said. "Miss Josie and Mr. Jeet would be the best guardians ever."

"But he didn't say yes," Jessie said. "He's going to think about it. Miss Josie asked him again to stay at least until the marathon."

"Why would he want to leave all this?" Hyacinth said, gesturing at the city spread out around them.

"This *is* the best place in the whole entire world to live," Isa said.

"He misses Georgia, though," Oliver said. "He always talks about football and the warm weather."

"And the food," Laney added. "Biscuits and fried chicken and collard greens."

The Vanderbeekers thought for a moment.

"Maybe we can make this place more like home to him," Isa began.

"Let's get him season tickets to the Knicks," Oliver suggested. "He would have to live here to see all the games."

"I think that's what *you* want, Oliver," Jessie said.

"He wants to make money," Isa said, ignoring her brother. "Maybe we can find him a job."

"Isn't he too young to work?" Jessie asked.

"Benny works," Laney said. Benny was Isa's friend from school, and he worked at Castleman's Bakery.

"That's because it's a family business," Jessie explained. "When you're working for your parents, you can start when you're twelve."

"Hmm," Isa said, pulling out her phone. "Let me check the laws." She opened up her internet browser and searched for labor laws in New York City. "It says here that he can get his working papers. He needs to go to the guidance counselor at school and get a form signed."

Jessie took the phone from Isa and skimmed the information. "But it says here that you need the signature of a parent or guardian. He also needs a passport or a birth certificate."

"Maybe Orlando can get a job where he doesn't need working papers," Isa said. "Like babysitting or dog walking."

"He really likes animals," Laney said, thinking about how good he was with their pets.

"Lots of people need dog walkers," Hyacinth added.

"We could advertise at the cat café," Isa said. "What do you think, Jessie?"

Jessie had been staring at the New York City skyline. "What?"

"About trying to get Orlando a job as a dog walker," Hyacinth explained with infinite patience.

"Oh, sure," Jessie said. "I can help him walk dogs."

"Perfect," Isa said. "Now, what else?"

The Vanderbeekers continued to brainstorm for another thirty minutes. Hyacinth was worried that Orlando didn't like New York City's brisk winters, so she put herself in charge of making Orlando lots of warm clothes. She was going to ask Herman Huxley for help because he was a great—and fast—knitter. Isa planned to enlist Allegra to help make posters advertising Orlando's dog-walking services, and Oliver offered to look into football programs nearby. Laney was going to help decorate Orlando's room and make sure he had as many cookies as he wanted and that he never went hungry.

"What about you, Jessie?" Hyacinth asked. "What do you want to do?"

When Jessie didn't respond right away, Laney jumped in. "You probably don't need to do anything extra. Papa always says that friendship is the best gift, and since you're his best friend, you're already giving him the best gift in the world."

Jessie nodded, but Isa couldn't help feeling that her twin didn't believe a word Laney had just said.

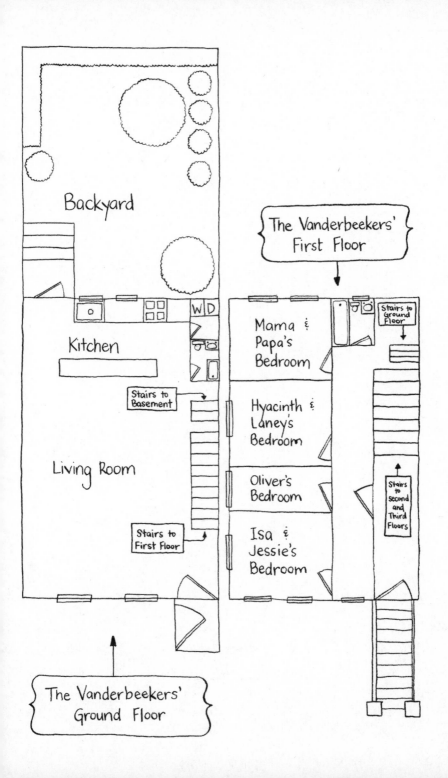

MONDAY, OCTOBER 21

Thirteen Days Until the New York City Marathon

Eight

On Monday morning, Oliver met Jimmy L and Angie, his best friends, outside school.

"Why did you want us here so early?" Jimmy L asked, shivering in the morning cold. None of them were ready to lug around their heavy winter coats yet, so they wore only hoodies. "It was torture waking up this morning."

"Orlando needs our help," Oliver said, and immediately his friends snapped to attention.

"Is he in trouble?" Angie asked.

"What do we need to do?" Jimmy L asked, suddenly awake.

"He might be going back to Georgia," Oliver explained, "so we need to find reasons for him to stay.

He talks about missing football, and since his high school doesn't have a team, I thought we could talk to Coach Mendoza about ideas."

Coach Mendoza had been their PE teacher for the last four years, and he was pretty much the coolest human being alive. Even Herman, who didn't like sports, liked going to PE. Coach Mendoza made everyone feel good regardless of their athletic ability and was always shouting words of encouragement.

Oliver, Jimmy L, and Angie liked Coach Mendoza in particular not only because was he an awesome basketball player, but because he had been a Navy SEAL before becoming a teacher. If being an NBA basketball player didn't work out for Oliver, he planned to follow in Coach Mendoza's footsteps and become a Navy SEAL.

The group entered the school and jogged toward the gym. The hallways were absolutely deserted, with the exception of a few blurry-eyed teachers cradling cups of coffee. When Oliver opened the door to the gym, however, a blast of music hit their ears.

Inside, Coach Mendoza was leading a group of high schoolers in what looked like tryouts for a junior extreme sports reality show. The teenagers were booking it back and forth across the gymnasium, their sneakers sliding and squeaking against the ground so fast that they were a blur.

When Coach Mendoza saw his visitors, he smiled and turned down the music.

"Take five," he yelled to the runners. A few of them dropped to the ground to catch their breath while another group dragged themselves toward the water fountains.

"What brings you here so early?" Coach Mendoza asked Oliver, Angie, and Jimmy L.

"We need your advice," Oliver said. "Our friend Orlando Stewart goes to Powell with Jessie and Isa. He loves football, but their school doesn't have a team, and we thought you might have some ideas about a team he can play for."

"I know Orlando," Coach Mendoza said. "He was in my class last year. Big guy. Super nice. Hard worker."

"Yep," Oliver, Angie, and Jimmy L said.

"He's a natural athlete," their coach continued. "So, football, huh? Has he played before?"

Oliver nodded. "He played down in Georgia, but he hasn't played since he moved here. He's running cross-country right now. Do you want to see a video of him playing? I can get one for you."

"Cool, cool," Coach Mendoza said. "Well, he's got some options. There's a team here called the Harlem Jets that participates in the citywide football league. The head coach is a buddy of mine. If you send me the video, I'll pass it along. They're already in the middle of their season, but sometimes kids drop out halfway through, so there might be spots."

"Great!" Oliver said.

Coach Mendoza looked at his watch. "School doesn't start for another half hour. Want to do some training with my high school team? Last year they placed first in their division. See if you like it; maybe you'll want to join in a few years."

"Of course we're going to like it," Angie said, dropping her backpack and peeling off her track pants to reveal basketball shorts underneath.

"Do we want to win a million dollars?" Jimmy L said, following Angie's lead.

Oliver joined his friends on the court and did some quick jumping jacks and stretches; then Coach Mendoza called his players back onto the court.

"All right. Dribbling races!" Coach Mendoza called. His high schoolers groaned, but Oliver, Angie, and Jimmy L cheered. They loved dribbling races.

"I've got some new blood to get you guys moving," Coach Mendoza said, pointing at his middle schoolers. "Let's start easy. Go down the court with right-hand dribbles, then back with your left. After that, crossover moves, and then dribbling with two basketballs. Ready?"

"Ready!" yelled Oliver, Jimmy L, and Angie.

The high schoolers rolled their eyes at their enthusiasm but crouched at the starting line.

Coach Mendoza blew his whistle, and off they went.

✹ ✹ ✹

Hyacinth didn't like being early to school. Her ideal arrival time was three minutes before the bell rang. That was just long enough that the class wouldn't leave for the classroom without her, but not too much time that she had to hang around feeling awkward if no one spoke to her.

Hyacinth had had the same two best school friends since kindergarten. She liked the familiarity and comfort of having two people she could hang out with at recess and lunch. She always got a little nervous talking to people she didn't know very well (which was pretty much everyone else in her grade), so it was excellent to have two best friends handy. But over the summer, one of her friends had switched schools, and her other friend had moved to New Jersey.

As a result, it was no surprise that the school year had not gotten off to a good start. Hyacinth used to like school okay, but now, with no friends, she pretty much dreaded it. Her teacher had already called her parents twice about the need for Hyacinth to participate more in class.

Hyacinth couldn't help that she felt comfortable only around her closest friends, which had now dwindled down to her siblings, Herman Huxley, and Orlando. Unfortunately, none of them was in her grade at school.

And now she was at school because Isa had an orchestra rehearsal and needed to drop Oliver, Hyacinth, and Laney off early. This worked out great for Oliver, who wanted to see Coach Mendoza before school began, but not so great for Hyacinth. She tried to convince Jessie to walk her to school instead so she could arrive at her regular three-minutes-before-the-bell, but her sister had woken up so grouchy that Hyacinth didn't want to ask for any favors.

Oliver ran off with his friends to the gym, so Hyacinth dropped Laney off in the kindergarten classroom, then dragged her feet down the hallway into the brightly lit cafeteria, which was where kids in first through fifth grades had to wait until school started. Given that she was forty-five minutes early, she was surprised to see she was not the first person to arrive. Dozens of kids were already there, clustered around the serving area. Hyacinth peeked around the crowd and saw that they were getting breakfast. She'd had no idea you could get breakfast at school.

Having eaten at home, Hyacinth headed toward one of the empty tables assigned to the third graders and sat down. She wished she had brought her knitting needles; she really needed to work on the quilt if she wanted to give it to Orlando by the day of the marathon. Instead, she took out a book and buried her head in it, hoping no one would notice her.

A few minutes later, a girl in her class named Maria sat across from her. Hyacinth peeked at her from behind her book. Maria wore her hair in pigtails and had glasses with thick red plastic frames perched on her nose. Her tray held french toast sticks, fruit, and a glass of orange juice.

"Hi, Hyacinth!" said Maria with a smile.

Hyacinth unburied her face from her book.

"Are you hungry?" Maria asked. "I got extra french toast sticks if you want one."

Hyacinth glanced at Maria's plate and shook her head. "I already ate."

Maria shrugged, then went back to her food. "Okay."

Hyacinth stared at the words in her book, but she wasn't reading them. She was thinking about what she could say to Maria. She wanted to ask why Maria ate breakfast at school instead of home and whether the french toast sticks were good. But before she could get the courage to look up from her book and say something, three more people from her class sat at the table. Maria started chatting with them, and pretty soon Hyacinth was back to being invisible.

Hyacinth didn't know why no one else in her family had problems talking to people. She thought longingly of Laney, who felt completely comfortable chatting with strangers on the subway, and Orlando, who had been living in Harlem for only a year and a half and already had tons of friends. He could talk to random people on the street and it didn't make him anxious at all.

Hyacinth wanted to be more like that. Could Orlando help her? Maybe he could teach her to be more like him. And maybe, if he knew how much she needed him, he would stay here forever and never go back to Georgia.

Nine

Jessie couldn't avoid Orlando at school. They shared most of their classes, which until today had been great. Now it was awkward. Orlando acted as if nothing had happened over the weekend, and he talked to her and joked around during class like he always did. Jessie, on the other hand, felt as if a rock were lodged in her throat. She knew Orlando needed her support, but she had so many feelings, and when she tried to say something to him, the words felt stuck.

In biology class, they sat at their lab table, listening to Ms. Brown talk about plant cells. After her lecture, she passed out worksheets that they had to complete in pairs.

Orlando's eyes lit up. "I love worksheets," he said, pulling a pen from his backpack and inching his stool closer to Jessie's.

Jessie rolled her eyes. "It's unnatural to *enjoy* doing worksheets."

"Nah," Orlando said. "Worksheets are awesome." He rubbed his hands together. "This one is fun. We need to draw organelles from plant cells and animal cells. I could do this in my sleep."

Jessie busied herself getting a pencil from her pencil case. What was wrong with him? Wasn't he traumatized by what had happened with his mom? While her best friend seemed thrilled to draw organelles, she agonized over whether he would still be here in two weeks.

"Plant cells have chloroplasts, a cell wall, and only one vacuole," Orlando said. "I'll draw the plant cells, you can do the animal cells. You should label everything, since you have better handwriting." He slid the worksheet between them so they could both access it.

Jessie glanced at the worksheet and started drawing in the animal-cell organelles. She got so involved in

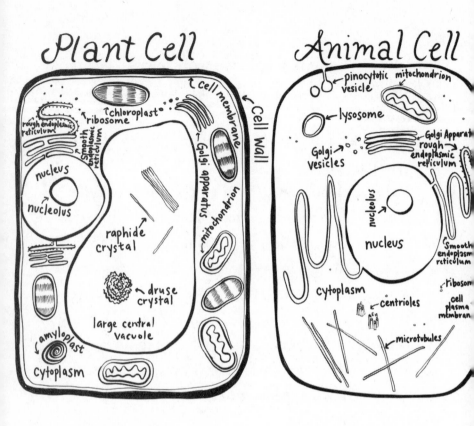

Plant Cell

- cell membrane
- chloroplast
- ribosome
- rough endoplasmic reticulum
- smooth endoplasmic reticulum
- nucleus
- nucleolus
- Golgi apparatus
- Cell Wall
- mitochondrion
- raphide crystal
- druse crystal
- large central vacuole
- amyloplast
- cytoplasm

Animal Cell

- pinocytotic vesicle
- mitochondrion
- lysosome
- Golgi Apparatus
- Golgi vesicles
- rough endoplasmic reticulum
- nucleolus
- nucleus
- Smooth endoplasmic reticulum
- cytoplasm
- ribosome
- cell plasma membrane
- centrioles
- microtubules

penciling in the blobs to look like mitochondria that she temporarily forgot about Orlando's situation.

"Maybe our science fair project should have something to do with cells," Jessie mused as she shaded in the mitochondria. "Like, I wonder if we can freeze cells without them being damaged."

There was a pause before Orlando said, "That's a good idea."

And suddenly, the weight of the weekend crashed back down on Jessie. She put down her pencil.

"Are you going to be here for the science fair?" she asked, trying to keep her voice even. "Or are you going back to Georgia?"

Orlando didn't look up from his drawing. "I don't know."

"How can you not know?" Jessie demanded.

Orlando looked up at her. "I don't know," he said with more snap in his voice than usual. "I have to think about it."

"What's going on with your mom? How come I've never met her? Why does she keep leaving you?"

Orlando put down his pen and glanced around. "Jessie, do we have to do this now?"

"Didn't Miss Josie say you could stay with her permanently?" Jessie continued, not able to let herself stop.

"She did—" Orlando began. "Wait, how did you know that?"

Jessie fumbled with her pencil, which rolled off the table and onto the floor. "Didn't she say it during dinner?"

Orlando stared at her. "No, she didn't."

Having retrieved the pencil, Jessie stood up and bumped her head against the lab table. "Ouch! Okay, fine. I overheard you last night when I was going to the REP. And personally, I think it would be a great idea for you to stay here—"

"Jessie, it's complicated, okay?" Orlando interrupted. "If I go back, I'll be there when my mom gets back."

Jessie shook her head, confused at Orlando's logic. His mom had *abandoned* him. He had been living in a *garden shed*. Why wouldn't he want the security of living with Mr. Jeet and Miss Josie?

"We want you to be safe," Jessie said.

"Listen," Orlando said impatiently. "My mom isn't like your mom. She needs my help. And please don't get your family involved. I don't want them to know about this."

"Why not?" Jessie asked. "We all care about you. We want to help."

Orlando shook his head. "It's just—I mean—I don't want the whole world to know my business. My mom isn't a terrible person, but I feel like that's what people immediately think."

"You can't seriously be thinking about going back to Georgia, though. Why go to your Aunt Tammy's when you can stay here with us? I know you didn't like living with her."

Orlando leaned forward in his chair, locking his fingers behind his head. "Can we stop talking about this? I need to figure out what my mom is planning first. She needs my help."

"But what about *you*?" Jessie asked, her voice rising. "Don't *you* need help too? And what about us? What about Miss Josie and Mr. Jeet? We need you, and we would never, *ever* abandon you!"

"That's not fair," Orlando said, his voice rising to meet hers. "You can't possibly understand the situation."

Ms. Brown's voice rose over the chatter. "Jessie, Orlando? Everything okay?"

"Sure," said Jessie, flashing Ms. Brown a smile, then glaring at Orlando.

Orlando sighed, his anger deflating. "I haven't decided anything yet. I don't want to leave, but things are . . . complicated. Can we just be normal? I've got a lot on my mind. I can't worry about us, too."

Jessie nodded, but it wasn't okay. In her mind, she kept seeing that dark, dank shed. In her heart, she knew nothing would feel better until Orlando was permanently living in the brownstone, where they could make sure he was safe.

✵ ✵ ✵

That afternoon when the last bell rang, Oliver met Hyacinth outside her classroom. She was standing in the back, alone, while her classmates jostled and joked in front of her. Oliver jumped up and down on his sneakers, waving his hands at her, and when she spotted him her face broke into a big smile. Pushing her way to the front of the classroom, she said goodbye to her teacher, and Oliver led the way down to the kindergarten classrooms. Laney was surrounded by her whole class, her arms moving up and down as she told a story. When she spotted Oliver and Hyacinth, she hugged all of her friends and then her teacher before joining her siblings.

They walked through the school doors and into the cool autumn afternoon. Orlando was standing by an oak tree with golden leaves that fluttered in the breeze, a hand in one pocket of his jacket. When he saw them, he lifted his chin, and Laney sprinted toward him and launched herself into his arms.

"Hi, Orlando!" called Eliza, Tamir, Andrew, and Paige, kids from Hyacinth's grade who were leaving school behind them. Orlando gave them high fives as they passed by to get on the school buses.

Everyone in the third grade knew Orlando because once the year before he'd had a day off from school on the same day as Special Visitor's Day. Papa had had a meeting at work and Mama had to be at the bakery for a health department inspection, so Orlando had volunteered to be Hyacinth's Special Visitor. Unlike the other visitors, Orlando hadn't sat on the sidelines and chatted during recess. He'd joined the kids on the jungle gym and played the cat game with Hyacinth and her friends, and back in the classroom, he'd taught the kids football drills when they got antsy. Then he'd helped the teachers put up a new bulletin board.

Ever since that day, his appearance had been cause

for celebration. Whenever the third graders saw him, they flocked to him as if he were a professional NBA basketball player.

"Where's Isa?" Oliver asked when he reached Orlando. Isa usually picked them up on Mondays and walked them home.

"Mr. Van Hooten wanted her to come in for an extra lesson after school," Orlando said. "My cross-country practice doesn't start for another hour, so I said I'd swing by and walk you home."

"Hey," Oliver said as they headed for 141st Street. "I have the best news for you."

"Oh yeah?" Orlando said. "Tell me."

"Coach Mendoza said there's a football league in Harlem," Oliver told him. "We just need to send him a video of you playing football. I was thinking of that one video where the quarterback threw to you and you ran fifty-three yards to make a touchdown? That was epic."

"Um, sure," Orlando said, running his hands through his short locks.

"Isn't that great about the Harlem team?" Oliver continued.

Orlando glanced at Oliver. "Yeah, that's cool, man. Thanks."

"And another great thing happened today," Oliver continued. "Coach Mendoza let Jimmy L, Angie, and me train with his high school basketball team, and he said we could come back whenever we want to because his team doesn't want to be beat by middle schoolers and worked harder around us. So we're totally going to go to all their morning practices now."

Hyacinth looked at him with startled eyes. "Wait, does that mean I have to go to school early *every day* now?"

"Only three times a week," Oliver said. "Mondays, Tuesdays, and Thursdays."

"But I don't want to go in early," Hyacinth said. "I want to be there three minutes before the bell rings, like always. I hate waiting in the cafeteria."

"You could ask Jessie to take you," Oliver suggested.

"She's so grouchy in the mornings," Hyacinth said. "She'll say no."

"Aren't Malia and Lucy there?" Orlando asked.

Hyacinth shook her head. "They don't go to my

school anymore. It's just me now." She looked so forlorn that even Oliver felt bad for her, but not bad enough to give up an epic basketball opportunity.

"What about the other kids in your class? Have you made new friends?" Orlando asked.

"Not really," Hyacinth said. "I don't like talking to people I don't know."

"They're in your class," Oliver pointed out. "They're not strangers."

"I still don't like it," Hyacinth said, her lips pursed. "They don't like talking to me."

"That doesn't sound right," Orlando said. "You're a great friend. You're fun to be around, you're interesting, you're nice. What's not to like?"

Hyacinth shrugged. "I tried to talk to a girl in my class before school this morning, but right before I was going say something, a bunch of people came over."

"You could have still talked to her," Oliver said.

"I don't like talking when there's a lot of people around," Hyacinth said. "Sometimes I say something and people ignore me and then it makes me not want to talk. I'm not like you. Everyone loves you immediately."

Orlando smiled down at Hyacinth and ruffled her hair. "It's okay to be quiet and enjoy time by yourself, but it sounds like you miss having a couple of really good friends."

Hyacinth thought about it. "I don't need a lot of friends, but it would be nice to have one or two."

Orlando nodded. "Why don't we work on that? You know, I used to be shy when I was little."

Hyacinth, Laney, and Oliver's mouths dropped open.

"*You* used to be shy?" Hyacinth said.

"Yep," Orlando said. "That's why I can help you. I've got a tried-and-true recipe for success. We just need to give you some confidence."

Hyacinth was skeptical. "I don't think that will work."

Oliver looked at Hyacinth. "I don't know why you need confidence. You're the coolest person."

Hyacinth's eyes grew wide with wonder. She pointed to herself. "Me?"

"Yeah," Oliver said, as if it were the most obvious thing in the world.

Orlando clapped a hand on Oliver's shoulder. "We're going to get Hyacinth filled with confidence in no time!" He turned toward Hyacinth.

Hyacinth swallowed.

"Your first lesson," Orlando told her, "is tonight after dinner. Be ready."

Ten

When she arrived home, Laney immediately packed Paganini in his carrier, picked up Tuxedo and settled him around her shoulders like a neck pillow, and headed upstairs to Miss Josie and Mr. Jeet's place. The nice thing about wearing turtlenecks was that they protected her skin from Tuxedo's claws.

Ms. Geraldine, Laney's least favorite of the three nurses who took care of Mr. Jeet, opened the door before Laney even made it to the top of the steps.

"Shhhh," Ms. Geraldine said, holding a finger to her lips.

"How did you know it was me?" Laney asked, hopping up the final three steps.

"Because you are very loud," Ms. Geraldine said.

"Hmph," Laney said, annoyed. Mr. Jeet, Miss Josie, *and* Mr. Beiderman never complained that she was loud. She walked into the apartment as quietly as she could and found Mr. Jeet napping in his hospital bed.

"He's resting, so don't bother him," Ms. Geraldine said, her eyes narrowed.

Laney glowered back at her. Mr. Jeet was Laney's best friend; she knew how to treat him when he was tired! She slipped by, hoping Ms. Geraldine wouldn't notice her bag.

"And do not take that rabbit from your bag," Ms. Geraldine continued. "It is very disruptive, and I don't want to clean up after that dirty animal."

Rabbits are very clean! Laney wanted to protest. But instead she (quietly) shuffled her way to the living room and sat down in the big armchair that had been Mr. Jeet's favorite until recently. These days, Mr. Jeet was either in bed or in his wheelchair, no more sitting in his favorite dark-green armchair with the tiny white flowers. Laney snuggled into the chair, pulled her turtleneck up to her mouth, and chewed on it. Tuxedo unwrapped herself from Laney's neck and jumped down to inspect Billie Holiday's ears.

Because Laney wasn't allowed to let Paganini out, she kept the bag on her lap, zipped up. She turned her head to one side and breathed in. She could smell Mr. Jeet's familiar scent, a combination of gardens and clean, good earth. It reminded her of the community garden, and she wondered if she could take Mr. Jeet there that weekend. Orlando would have to help carry him downstairs, which made Laney wonder what would happen if Orlando left to go back to Georgia. What would Mr. Jeet and Miss Josie do without his help?

Mr. Jeet stirred and opened his eyes, and Laney stood and put Paganini's carrier on the bed. Then she climbed up next to Mr. Jeet and squeezed his hand.

"Hi, Mr. Jeet," she said.

He waved the fingertips of his left hand weakly.

Footsteps came from the kitchen, and the nurse tsked at Laney. "No, no, Lulu, give Mr. Jeet some space."

"It's *Laney*," Laney said.

Mr. Jeet waved Ms. Geraldine's concerns away and shook his head, and Ms. Geraldine started to protest.

"He likes it when I sit here," Laney said. "He

doesn't want me to leave; that's what he's trying to tell you. I know, because he's my best friend and I've known him my whole life."

"Fine, fine," the nurse said, turning and heading back to sit at the dining room table. "Just be careful!"

Laney yanked up her turtleneck and bit down on it hard. Of course she'd be careful! She wished Ms. Geraldine would leave them alone. She turned to Mr. Jeet, who waved in the direction of Paganini's case.

"Do you want him to come out?" she asked, her hand going to the zipper.

Mr. Jeet nodded.

Laney glanced uneasily at Ms. Geraldine, who was absorbed in something on her phone. Seeing that the nurse was preoccupied, Laney unzipped her bag. Paganini bounded out with a flourish and looked around to see where he was. Recognizing Mr. Jeet, he hopped a few paces forward and rested his front feet and chin on Mr. Jeet's chest. Billie Holiday sat by the hospital bed and let out a big sigh at the injustice of a rabbit being on the bed when she had to stay on the floor.

"I was thinking," Laney said as she stroked Paganini's head, "that you haven't seen the garden lately. Mr.

Jones has a mystery plant! It came out of his planter even though he didn't plant it, and no one knew what it was but he figured he would let it grow and see what happens. He calls it his bonus plant. Now it's a long vine creeping along the ground like a monster. And last week a thing that looks like a pumpkin started growing on the vine, but instead of being orange and bumpy it's green and very smooth. Jessie and Orlando tried to figure out what it is from the internet. I'm pretty sure if you took one look at it you could tell what it is."

Mr. Jeet gave her a half smile, then looked as if he was going to say something. Laney held her breath and listened really hard, but nothing came out of his mouth. Then he closed his eyes and fell asleep. Laney sat back, disappointed.

The click of a door revealed Miss Josie emerging from the bathroom. She was wrapped in a beautiful floral bathrobe, and her hair was in curlers underneath her shower cap.

"How nice to see you, Laney," she said, smiling wide. "How are you doing today?"

Laney hopped off the bed and gave Miss Josie a big

hug. "I'm good. Do you think Mr. Jeet can come to the garden this weekend? I have so much to show him."

"Oh, honey, I'm not sure," Miss Josie said. "I would love to bring him, but he has been really tired lately, and it's quite cold outside."

Laney pulled at her turtleneck, fidgeting with the hem. "Maybe next week, then?"

"We'll see how he's feeling," Miss Josie said. "He needs a lot of rest these days, doesn't he? I know he appreciates you coming by every afternoon to keep him company."

"Of course," Laney said. "That's what best friends do, right?"

"We are so lucky to have you," Miss Josie said. "Now I have an idea: why don't I get us some afternoon tea?"

Laney nodded—she loved afternoon tea—and Miss Josie headed to the kitchen.

Ms. Geraldine came by and scowled at the sight of Paganini stretched out on the bed. "I've got to do Mr. Jeet's checkup," she said stiffly; then she pointed at Paganini as if he were a nest of fire ants. "Please put *that* away."

Laney scowled back, picked up Paganini, and placed him gently in his carrier. She set it on the floor next to Billie Holiday and Tuxedo and watched as Ms. Geraldine checked Mr. Jeet's blood pressure, temperature, and heart monitor. Laney kept peeking at the numbers, but she couldn't tell what anything meant. She pulled her turtleneck back up and retreated to the place where everything was fine and Mr. Jeet was healthy again and they didn't need mean nurses like Ms. Geraldine ordering them around.

✧ ✧ ✧

After her violin lesson with Mr. Van Hooten, Isa headed to the Treehouse Bakery to meet Allegra and work on the dog-walking posters.

She took her time making her way to the café from the music school. Autumn was her favorite season; the leaves had changed from their late-summer dark-green color to a mix of burgundies, oranges, and golds. The cool breeze blew through her hair, and she took a deep breath and appreciated how the crisp air filled her lungs and made everything feel fresh and new.

Isa hitched the strap of her violin case higher on

her shoulder. As she passed a tan brownstone with ivy creeping up the bricks, she realized she was walking along 139th Street. Benny's apartment was on the opposite side of the street. That reminded her to ask him about the homecoming dance, which was the Saturday before the marathon.

She had gone to last year's homecoming with Benny when she was in eighth grade and he was a freshman in high school, though it was still a mystery why there was a homecoming dance at all since Powell High School didn't even have a football team.

Isa thought about stopping by his place, but she needed to get to the café, and Benny worked at his parents' bakery on Mondays anyway. As she got closer to the middle of the block, she glanced across the street and saw Benny sitting on a bench in front of his building. He must have had an unexpected day off.

She was about to call out to him and cross the street to say hello, but then she realized he wasn't alone.

Sitting next to him was a girl she had never seen before.

Eleven

Isa didn't stop walking. She trained her eyes forward and kept going until she passed the bench, hoping Benny wouldn't notice her. When she got to the end of the block, she slowed down, let out a breath, and looked back, peeking around a silver minivan to get another look at Benny and the mystery girl. There they were, sitting together on the bench, paying no attention to her or to anyone else. Isa hadn't recognized the girl in that brief glance when she'd walked by, and now she was too far away to see clearly.

Who was she? And why was Benny sitting with her? Isa watched for a few minutes, then she reluctantly turned the corner and made her way toward the café. Three kittens that had arrived the previous day were snoozing in a hammock in front of the large window seat.

Allegra was already there, leaning over the counter and chatting with Jason, one of the cashiers. Jason was a junior at their high school, and Allegra had a huge crush on him.

Purl One scampered up and gave a squeaky *meow* when Isa entered the café. After resting her backpack and violin by a table, Isa picked up Purl One and cradled the cat to her chest, trying to get some comfort from the rumbly purrs.

"Hey, girl," Allegra said, setting two hot chocolates on the table. "Where've you been? Not that I'm complaining—I got to talk to Jason for four point three minutes. Do you think he likes me? Wait," Allegra said, putting her hands in front of her. "Don't answer that! I can't handle the truth. I will just sit here quietly and hold on to my impossible dream that he will ask me to homecoming. You're so lucky you have an automatic date to the dance."

Isa looked up at her friend. "I'm not so sure about that."

Allegra planted both hands on the table and leaned toward Isa. "Say again?"

"I just passed his apartment building, and he was hanging out with a girl."

"No!"

"Yes."

"You must be mistaken," Allegra said, pulling a chair out and sitting down. "It was Benny's evil twin brother. A look-alike. A doppelgänger. That definitely wasn't your Benny."

"It was definitely my Benny," Isa said, then rolled her eyes. "I mean, not *my* Benny. He's just . . . Ugh, I'm just trying to say that it *was* him. He doesn't belong to me. He's Benny. *Our* friend."

"Uh-huh," Allegra said, leaning back in her chair and crossing her arms. "I don't know why you're worried. He only has eyes for you. Anyway, you're going to homecoming with him, right?"

Isa looked away. "I *thought* so, but the thing is, I don't think he ever asked me. And I definitely never asked him."

"You've gone to every dance together for the past

two years," Allegra pointed out. "It's always been Isa and Benny, Benny and Isa."

"We're only friends," Isa insisted. "We don't have to go to every dance together. He can go with someone else."

"You're not just friends, you're best friends," Allegra said. "Which, by the way, I don't understand at all. I can be friends with boys, but I can't imagine being *best* friends with a boy."

Isa tried again. "He's Benny. We've known each other forever. I don't think of him as a boyfriend."

Allegra raised an eyebrow. "So you're telling me you have no romantic feelings for him at all."

"I don't think so," Isa said. "There are lots of things I want to do. Violin, orchestra, school. Having a boyfriend never seemed important."

Allegra looked disappointed. Thinking about boyfriends had always been a big part of her life. "Well, that stinks. I've already spent a lot of time designing my bridesmaid dress for your wedding with Benny. You're going to ask me to be a bridesmaid, right? My dress will be long, of course, with sparkly beading all over it so it will shimmer in the light . . ."

Isa listened halfheartedly as Allegra went on to describe what she envisioned the groomsmen wearing. At least listening to Allegra kept her from admitting how much it bothered her to see Benny with another girl.

❖ ❖ ❖

That night after dinner, Hyacinth and Laney headed up to Mr. Jeet and Miss Josie's apartment. Laney had brought supplies to decorate Orlando's room, and she was ready to learn everything there was to know about football. She was even wearing a Yankees cap for the occasion, and Hyacinth had tied a blue-and-orange scarf—Mets colors—around Franz's neck.

They brought a dozen assorted cookies from the café, which Oliver, in an heroic feat of sacrifice, had insisted they give to Orlando rather than eat for dessert. Oliver was, after all, in charge of making sure Orlando had all the food he wanted. Papa had figured out how to get Orlando's phone reconnected and had put him on the Vanderbeeker family phone plan so he wouldn't have to worry about the bills. Jessie had ordered everyone to keep Operation Save Orlando (OSO) under wraps, which meant Laney wasn't allowed to say anything about it to anyone but her siblings.

Hyacinth knocked on the door, and Ms. Fran, the nice nurse, opened the door. Laney gave her a hug.

"Hello, Hyacinth. Hello, Laney," Ms. Fran said in a whisper, opening the door wide. It was dim inside the apartment, with only one small kitchen light on.

"Is Mr. Jeet already asleep?" Hyacinth whispered back.

Ms. Fran nodded. "Miss Josie went to a church meeting. She'll be back in an hour. Orlando is in his room."

Hyacinth and Laney crept through the living room, peeking at Mr. Jeet as they passed him. Their neighbor was so still, multiple blankets covering him. Under the hospital bed lay Billie Holiday, her eyes roving around the room. Mr. Jeet looked as if he needed lots of sleep, so Hyacinth and Laney left him alone. Laney knocked on Orlando's door, and he opened it and let them in.

"I'm ready to watch football and decorate your room!" Laney said once the door was closed behind her.

"Right, football. So the first thing you should know is—" Orlando began, then said, "Wait, you want to decorate this room? Why?"

"To give it some pizzazz, of course!" Laney said.

Hyacinth looked around. The room still had lots of Miss Josie and Mr. Jeet's things in it, including multiple wall hangings, a heavy wooden desk as big as a taxi, a large vinyl chair, and lacy curtains.

Orlando raised an eyebrow. "Really?"

"Yep," Laney said, standing up on the bed and taping a purple crepe-paper streamer as high up the wall as she could reach. "We want to fix up your room so you'll be happy to live here."

"I'm happy to be here, but I'd rather we leave the room the way it is," Orlando said. "I don't want to move their stuff around. I'm just here temporarily."

"Oh!" said Hyacinth. "I almost forgot. Papa got your phone connected again. He put you on our family plan."

Orlando frowned. "He didn't have to do that. That's expensive."

"But if you don't have a phone, how will we contact you?" Hyacinth asked. "What if your mom needs to call you?"

Orlando shook his head, but he pulled his phone from his small outside pocket. He turned it on, and the reception bars popped up. Hyacinth looked over his shoulder and saw a few text messages flash on the screen, all of them from Jessie.

JESSIE: Hey, my dad said he got your phone working again.

JESSIE: No ignoring me now, ha. Not that you would ever do that. Wait, would you ever do that?

JESSIE: Let me know when you get this so we know it's working.

Orlando typed a short message back to Jessie, then shoved his phone into his pocket. Laney put up another streamer, a pink one with unicorns galloping across it.

"Are these streamers from your birthday party?" Orlando asked.

"Yes," Laney said. "I had them hanging up in my room, but I thought you might need them more."

He cleared his throat, then looked at Hyacinth. "Do you want to learn about football too?"

Hyacinth shook her head. "Not really."

"Orlando's favorite team is the Hawks," Laney said with authority.

"Not the Hawks, the Falcons," Orlando said. "The Atlanta Falcons."

"Yep," Laney said, nodding knowledgeably.

"Bad news, Laney Bean," Orlando said. "The only TV is in the living room, and Mr. Jeet is sleeping."

"Let's go to our apartment," Laney said.

"You guys don't even have a TV," Orlando pointed out. "But there's another game later this week. We can watch it then."

"Okay," Laney said. "I want to watch them make home runs."

Orlando rubbed his temples with index and middle fingers. "Home runs are for baseball. In *football,* they score by making touchdowns or field goals. But it's fine . . . we'll cover all that. Hey, since you're here . . ."

Orlando said, looking at Hyacinth, "maybe we should work on *your* mission: making friends."

"Ooh," Laney interjected. She was done hanging the streamers, but she continued to bounce on the bed, her pigtails swinging from side to side as she jumped. "I love making friends. It's my favorite thing to do."

She glanced at her sister, but Hyacinth looked less than thrilled.

"Tomorrow is Tuesday," Hyacinth said quietly, "so we don't have to go in early. I don't have to worry about talking to people until Wednesday."

"So we'll practice tomorrow," Orlando said. "I'll walk you to school."

"Do I have to talk to complete strangers?" Hyacinth asked, biting her pinky finger. "I don't think I can talk to complete strangers."

"Tell them you like their shoes," Laney suggested. "People love it when you compliment their shoes."

"You're a six-year-old genius," Orlando said to Laney before turning back to Hyacinth. "It won't be scary at all. I'll be with you the entire time."

Hyacinth did not look convinced. "Now I'm *more* worried."

Orlando turned to Laney. "Tell your sister there's nothing to worry about."

"There's nothing to worry about," Laney said, falling to the bed and rolling around so Orlando's comforter wrapped around her like a taco shell. "You should trust Orlando. He knows *a lot*. Especially about football and home runs, but about other things too."

The thing was, Hyacinth *did* trust Orlando. She just didn't trust herself.

Twelve

Jessie sat at her desk in her bedroom, staring at her phone and willing Orlando to call or text. She had received a brief "Thanks" after the texts she had sent him that afternoon. But after that, nothing.

Her bedroom door opened, and Oliver appeared. He entered without an invitation, heading straight toward her and plucking the phone from her hand.

"Hey!" Jessie said, swatting him to get it back.

Oliver plugged in the password to unlock her phone, then started scrolling through her photos.

"How do you know my password?" Jessie exclaimed.

"I've known it forever," Oliver said. "How do you

think all those photos of the inside of Franz's ear end-ed up on here?"

"Those were Franz's ears?" Jessie asked. "That's disgusting."

"I prefer 'artistic genius,'" Oliver said, continuing to scroll.

"Oliver, seriously, give me back my phone. I'm expecting a call."

"I just need . . . Aha! I'm going to send this off and . . . done." Oliver handed the phone back to her.

"You didn't just hack into a government computer or something, did you?" Jessie asked suspiciously.

"Nope," Oliver said. "I was looking for that football video of Orlando so I could send it to Coach Mendoza. He's going to show it to the coach of the Harlem Jets and get Orlando on the local football team."

Oliver left her bedroom, and Jessie checked her phone again—no messages—and considered whether she should text Orlando again. She didn't want to seem pushy, but on the other hand, she wanted to make sure he was okay. Had he heard from his mom now that his phone was reconnected?

Jessie drummed her fingers on the desk. It was quiet in the brownstone. With the exceptions of Oliver and Isa, who was practicing the violin, her siblings had headed to bed, and her parents were downstairs watching a movie on Papa's computer. She could hear faint violin music drifting up from the basement. Jessie's homework was done, and there was nothing to distract her from worrying about Orlando.

Jessie stood up and paced, then looked at her phone again. Nothing. *This is stupid,* Jessie thought. She had never worried about contacting Orlando before. If she wanted to talk to him, she was going to talk to him. And now that he lived in the apartment above her, she could go up and visit him whenever she wanted.

Not wanting to disturb Miss Josie and Mr. Jeet, Jessie decided to go the fire-escape route. She grabbed a hoodie and climbed out her window. The metal creaked as she stepped onto the platform, and she held the slim handrails as she went upstairs to the second floor. The window outside the living room was dark, but there was a light on in Orlando's room. His window was closed and the curtains were drawn, but there was a slim opening in the curtains where she could peek through to see if he was there.

Jessie crouched and looked through the curtains. Orlando was sitting at Miss Josie's big wooden desk, its drawers so stuffed with papers they didn't close all the way. A crystal vase of dusty silk flowers stood in one corner, a stack of Orlando's schoolbooks in the opposite corner. Orlando wasn't studying, though. He was just sitting there, staring at his phone on the desk. He wasn't flipping through it or writing an email or a text; he was just gazing at the dark screen, the way Jessie had been gazing at hers just a few minutes earlier. At the sight of him so forlorn, Jessie felt her heart squeeze. She decided then and there that she was going to stop being mad at Orlando for not telling her about his situation. Instead, she would be the best friend she could.

Jessie gently tapped her knuckles against the glass. A few seconds later, the window creaked open.

"Hey," Orlando said.

Jessie smiled. "Just checking in. Can I come in?"

"Actually, let's go outside," Orlando said. "I need some fresh air."

"Sure," Jessie said, moving aside to give him space.

Orlando bent down and squeezed through the small window and onto the fire escape. "Let's go to the roof; this fire escape won't hold me."

Jessie rolled her eyes. "I have no idea why you worry so much about the fire escape, but sure, let's go upstairs. The Adirondack chairs are more comfortable anyway."

On the roof, they settled into their favorite chairs: orange for Jessie and green for Orlando. It was chilly, so Jessie pulled her hoodie up, leaned back, and looked at the starless sky.

After a few minutes of silence, Orlando started to talk.

"I tried calling my mom's number," Orlando said. "I called eight times. It went to voicemail every single time."

Jessie turned to him. "Maybe she tried calling you when your phone was disconnected? Now that it's working again, I'm sure she'll get in touch soon."

Orlando shook his head. "I don't know. I keep waiting for her to contact me. I sent a text to your mom and dad, though. Guess how long it took them to respond?"

Jessie waited.

"Ten seconds." He stood up and walked to the edge of the roof and faced south. A glow of lights from Times Square and the tall office buildings of Midtown illuminated the night. "It was like they were waiting by their phones, hoping to hear that I was okay."

Jessie got up, made her way to Orlando, and put her arm around his waist. "I'm sorry."

He shook his head. "Don't be sorry. I'm not saying it to make you feel bad."

"Do you think she's okay?" Jessie asked. "Maybe she's sick or in the hospital."

Orlando shook his head. "She just . . . disappears sometimes. Do you know what she said to me once?" He paused and looked up. "She told me she never wanted to be a mom."

Jessie stared at him. His profile was dark against the night sky. "Wow."

Orlando nodded.

Jessie leaned her head on his shoulder. "Any mom would be lucky to have you as a son."

"Yeah," Orlando said, but he didn't sound convinced.

Later, after Jessie had said goodbye to Orlando and slipped back into her room, her parents poked their heads in to say goodnight.

"Good night, honey," Papa said, stepping inside to give her a hug.

"We love you," Mama said, putting an arm around her.

Jessie wasn't a big hugger, like Laney, Hyacinth, and Isa were; she merely tolerated her family's displays of physical affection. They called her the Leaner: someone who leans into a hug but doesn't actively participate in it. But tonight, she opened her arms wide and hugged her parents close to her heart, feeling grateful to be held tight on that chilly autumn night.

TUESDAY, OCTOBER 22

Twelve Days Until the New York City Marathon

Thirteen

Isa woke up on Tuesday and looked out the window. It was gloomy and cloudy, the kind of day that made her want to burrow under warm covers and listen to music on her headphones all day long. She did not want to get out of bed, she did not want to go to school, and she certainly did not want to come face-to-face with Benny Castleman. Somehow she felt as if nothing between them would ever be the same.

Willing herself out of bed, Isa glanced at her sister. Jessie was still sleeping, her comforter on the floor, her head under her pillow. "Jess, time to get up."

"Urghmf," Jessie replied.

Isa shrugged and headed down the hallway. Laney,

wearing a pair of black cat ears, was hopping from foot to foot in front of the bathroom.

"Who's in there?" Isa asked.

"Oliver!" Laney squeaked as she bounced. "And I really, really, really have to go!"

"Use the downstairs bathroom."

Laney shook her head vigorously. "Papa's taking a shower."

Isa rapped her knuckles on the door. "Oliver!"

"What?" yelled Oliver.

"There's a line out here," Isa yelled back. "Hurry up."

A few seconds later, the toilet flushed and the faucet turned on.

"It's a 'mergency!" Laney yelped.

Finally, the door opened and a rumpled Oliver came out with a copy of *The Serpent's Secret* in his hand. Laney raced past him into the bathroom, and Isa closed the door for her. Then she turned to Oliver.

"Really? Reading in the bathroom?"

"I was at a good part," Oliver said with a shrug.

"No reading in the bathroom!" Isa scolded him just

as Mama came out of her room, her hair as disheveled as Oliver's.

"I agree with Isa one thousand percent," she said, rubbing her eyes.

"Yeah, yeah," Oliver said, shuffling into his bedroom and closing the door.

Laney emerged, looking infinitely more relaxed. She had her toothbrush in one hand and Isa's toothbrush in the other. Isa squeezed a small glob of toothpaste onto both of their brushes. As they brushed, Isa examined herself in the mirror. Her hair was stringy and flat against her head, and for a moment she wished for Allegra's beautiful, voluminous hair. There were bags under Isa's eyes and a red mark on the left side of her neck, right under her chin, where her violin had rubbed against it over the years.

Isa had never spent a lot of time thinking about her appearance. Allegra was the fashionista, and Isa was a residual beneficiary of her friend's expertise. If Isa needed something to wear for a special occasion, Allegra was always ready with multiple suggestions from her own closet. Now, however, Isa wondered if she should be paying more attention to how she looked.

Isa felt a pull on her arm and looked down. Laney was pointing to her frothing mouth, toothpaste bubbles spilling out both sides.

"Oh my gosh," Isa said around her own mouthful of toothpaste. "Yes, go ahead and spit. You're done."

Isa waited for Laney to spit and rinse her toothbrush, then did the same.

"Double piggyback to the kitchen?" Laney asked, flashing her a beseeching grin.

Isa looked down at her little sister and smiled. "Of course."

Laney squealed with excitement, picked up Tuxedo, and wrapped the cat around her neck. Then Isa leaned down so Laney could hop onto her back. Together they went down the stairs, Laney making cat chirping sounds and Tuxedo purring loudly, following the smell of coffee brewing and whole-wheat apple-cranberry muffins baking. And for one moment Isa's heart grew lighter; she was glad that no matter how weird things got at school and with Benny, she could count on home and her family, always.

✦ ✦ ✦

Oliver, Hyacinth, and Laney headed to school that morning with Orlando and Isa. Isa offered to bring them by herself, but Orlando insisted on coming along. He had things to discuss with Hyacinth.

Isa watched as Oliver hitched his backpack higher on his shoulders and dribbled his basketball down the sidewalk, expertly navigating it around the uneven cracks.

"You're going to talk to Coach Mendoza, right?" Oliver said to Orlando. "He can help you get on the Harlem Jets."

"I'm already pretty busy with cross-country," Orlando said. "I don't know if I can do football too."

"But you love football," Oliver said, bouncing the basketball off the lid of a trash can on the curb, then catching it.

"I do love it," Orlando said. "But I'm committed to

my cross-country team, and I told Mr. B I would help him train for the marathon."

Oliver frowned. "If you were in Georgia, you'd be on the football team."

"Yeah," Orlando agreed. "But I'm not in Georgia."

"I already told Coach Mendoza that you would talk to him, though," Oliver said.

Orlando sighed and looked at his watch. "I don't have time this morning. I've got science club right after I drop you off."

Oliver frowned and jogged to catch up with Laney and Hyacinth.

Isa sidled next to Orlando. "You feeling okay?"

"I haven't been sleeping so great," Orlando admitted.

"You've got a lot going on," Isa said. "I know you have Miss Josie to talk to, but remember, Jessie and I are great listeners."

"Don't worry about me," Orlando said. "I've been talking to both Miss Josie and Mr. Beiderman."

"We're here if you need us," Isa said.

Isa felt Orlando's eyes on her.

"You don't look like you slept well either."

Isa smoothed her hair. "Yeah. Hey, are you going to homecoming?"

Orlando shook his head. "I don't like dances."

"Why not?"

"It's not my thing," Orlando said. "But you're going, right? Don't you go to all the dances with Benny?"

Isa paused. "I think he wants to go with someone different this time."

Orlando frowned. "I don't know Benny that well, but that doesn't sound right. Maybe you should talk to him."

Isa breathed out. "That's a good idea. Thanks." She looked ahead to where Laney was running to catch up to a large garbage truck rolling down the street.

"Mr. Mark!" Laney yelled. The truck squealed to a stop, and Mr. Mark, who worked for the city sanitation department, hopped off the back.

"Hey, Laney!" Mr. Mark called out. "I've got a riddle for you. What starts with the letter 'T,' is filled with 'T,' and ends with 'T'?"

"Oh, I know!" Laney exclaimed. "Um, it's toot. Or a tart. No, that's not right. Filled with 'T'? What doess *that* mean?"

"Give up?" Mr. Mark asked.

"Nope," Laney said, and looked to her siblings for help.

"It's a teapot," Hyacinth whispered.

"Hyacinth knows!" Laney announced, tugging on her arm. "Hyacinth, tell him."

Hyacinth didn't say a word.

"Hyacinth, it's just Mr. Mark," Orlando said. "You can talk to him. Consider this practice."

Hyacinth shook her head again.

"You can do it," Isa said.

Hyacinth looked up briefly, then blurted out, "I like your shoes!"

There was brief silence as everyone glanced at Mr. Mark's scuffed sneakers; then Mr. Mark smiled at Hyacinth. "Thanks! These *are* good shoes!"

"The answer is a teapot!" Laney called out. "Hyacinth figured it out."

Mr. Mark laughed. "I can never trick Hyacinth." He hopped back onto the garbage truck and hit the side of the hopper to signal to the driver that he was ready to roll. "Have a great day!" he called as the truck roared down the street.

Orlando looked at Hyacinth and put his hand on her shoulder. "That was . . . great."

Isa nodded. "Good job, Hyacinth."

"I like how you complimented his shoes," Laney added.

Oliver didn't say a word.

"It was terrible!" Hyacinth said, covering her face with her hands.

"You just need practice," Orlando assured her. "Here's an assignment for you: at school this morning, I want you to ask someone three questions about themselves. People *love* talking about themselves."

"That is true," Laney said with an air of expertise.

Hyacinth shook her head. "No, thank you."

"How about we barter," Orlando suggested. "If you do it, I'll do something for you. Hey, you can teach me how to knit!"

Oliver made a face. "Honestly, Orlando, I think you're giving up too much."

Hyacinth looked at Orlando. "I'll try your plan for

now, but in return, you have to stay in Harlem forever."

"Yay!" Laney cheered.

Oliver whistled. "Master negotiator right there!"

Orlando ran his hand over his head and stopped at the entrance to the elementary school. "I can't make those types of promises, Hyacinth. I wish I could say for sure what I'll do, but I can't."

"Okay, then you'll have to promise to *strongly* consider staying here," Hyacinth said.

Orlando gave her a small smile. "I promise to *strongly* consider staying here."

Hyacinth stuck out her right hand and Orlando shook it. Then Hyacinth stood up tall, grabbed Laney's hand, and marched into school.

Fourteen

After Hyacinth dropped off Laney, she headed to the cafeteria. The third-grade tables were empty, but a bunch of people were getting breakfast. Hyacinth sat down and resisted the urge to pull out a book.

She drummed her fingers against the tabletop, waiting for someone else to sit down, hoping she didn't look as scared as she felt. A few minutes later, a whole group of her classmates—including Maria—headed in her direction, and Hyacinth swallowed the panic that filled her throat. She crossed her fingers under the table, hoping that Maria would take a seat next to her.

"Hi," Hyacinth said as they sat down at her table, Maria taking the seat the farthest away from her.

No one responded, and Hyacinth wasn't sure if that was because no one could hear her or because they didn't want to talk to her. She inched her way along the bench to get closer to them. It sounded as if they were arguing about the results of the soccer game at recess the day before.

"You only won because you cheated," Marcos said to Eliza.

"We didn't cheat!" Eliza said. "There's no rule against meowing like a kitten to distract your opponents!"

"It was weird," Maria said, taking a spoonful of her cereal. "You confused us."

"That was the point," Eliza said.

Marcos was closest to Hyacinth, and even though he wasn't Hyacinth's first choice of a person to talk to, due to his argumentative nature, she remembered her promise to Orlando. She took a deep breath and said, "Why do you eat breakfast here instead of at home?"

"Your whole team was making illegal moves," Marcos said to Eliza.

"Yeah," agreed Andrew. "You also grabbed my arm

when I had the ball. You're not supposed to do that."

Hyacinth coughed and leaned forward in hopes of attracting Marcos's attention. "Um, do you always eat your cereal without milk?"

"I call a rematch! Today, at recess!" Eliza announced.

"Yes! Rematch!" the rest of the kids chanted. "Rematch! Rematch!"

Hyacinth drooped in her seat. She had promised Orlando she was going to ask three questions, but Maria was all the way at the other end of the table, and she was the only person Hyacinth really wanted to talk to. So instead she whispered her last question so quietly that even she couldn't hear it against the roar of her classmates' chanting.

"Maria, do you want to be my friend?"

✧ ✧ ✧

When Isa arrived at school that morning, she beelined to her locker. Sometimes Benny met her there before class, but today he was nowhere to be seen. Isa sighed, then spun the dial on her combination lock. After changing her books out, she checked her phone to see if anyone had responded to the dog-walking posters.

"What's up?" Allegra said, coming up behind her.

"Just checking to see if anyone wrote to us about dog walking."

"Don't be stressed if no one has responded yet," Allegra said. "It takes time to build a client base. I should know. Remember my nail-painting business? I'd be a millionaire by now if Principal Reynolds hadn't shut it down."

"Hold up," Isa said, showing Allegra her phone. "Check out all these responses!"

Allegra squealed. "How many are there?"

"Thirty-two!"

"Holy smokes!" Allegra said. "Okay, here's what you do. First, ask them to come by the cat café this afternoon. Second, make sure Orlando is there, because once they meet him they'll totally want him to walk their dogs. Third, figure out a schedule and rates. Fourth, make all clients sign a contract."

"Wow, okay," Isa said, impressed by her friend's business savvy. "We don't have a contract, though."

"I'll make one at lunch," Allegra said. "Easy."

Isa typed out an email, blind copied all the people who had contacted her, and pressed send. "I hope people show up. If this works out, Orlando will be rich!"

Isa said goodbye to Allegra—they had different classes for first period—then spent the rest of morning trying not to think about Benny. It was Tuesday, so they had biology together after lunch. When she got to class, Isa sat at their usual lab table, one eye trained on the door. Ms. Brown was passing out the tests when Benny rushed in, flashing Isa a smile as he slid onto the stool next to her. She tried to smile back, but it felt more like a grimace. Benny didn't seem to notice. He had already pulled a pen out and started on his test.

Isa, on the other hand, had a hard time concentrating. She kept wanting to glance at Benny, but she didn't want Ms. Brown to think she was trying to cheat. The sheer amount of concentration it took to keep from looking over made her take a lot longer than usual to complete the test. Benny, however, was done twenty minutes before class was over and got permission to go to study hall for the rest of the period, while Isa had to rush through the last two pages to finish before the bell.

Benny was nowhere to be seen for the rest of the day, which simultaneously relieved and annoyed Isa. She knew she should talk to him about the dance, but at the same time, she thought it would be awkward. By the time the final bell rang, she was exhausted.

"What's wrong?" Jessie asked when she met Isa at her locker.

"Nothing," Isa said.

"Hey, ladies," Allegra said, running up to them and slinging one arm around each twin's shoulder. "Isa, what's with the sad face? This isn't about Benjamin, is it?"

"What happened with Benjamin?" Jessie asked.

"Isa caught him hanging out with another girl yesterday when he was *supposed* to be working," Allegra said in a conspiratorial whisper.

"So?" Jessie said with a shrug.

"So?" Allegra repeated, annoyed. "He only has eyes for Isa!"

Jessie shook her head. "Benjamin and Isa are best friends. It's not mushy romantic stuff."

"That's what I told her," Isa said quickly. "It's not a big deal."

Isa felt the penetrative gaze of her twin bore into her, and she occupied herself by flipping through the books in her locker.

Allegra spoke up. "Jessie, think about how it would feel if Orlando started hanging out with other girls."

Jessie stared back at Allegra. "It would feel . . . totally fine? Wait, was that a trick question?"

"All right, how about this: Are you going to homecoming?" Allegra asked.

"*Homecoming?* No," Jessie said with a shiver. "Blech."

Allegra tilted her head. "What are you going to do instead?"

"Work on my science fair project with Orlando."

"Ha!" Allegra said, raising her arms above her head as if she had won a critical debate. "You two are totally a couple."

"We're a couple because we're doing a science project together?" Jessie asked. "That makes no sense."

Isa closed her locker. Her bad mood had just turned from a light drizzle to storm clouds. Because the thing was, she had never thought of Benny as her boyfriend. So why couldn't she stop thinking about that girl he was hanging out with?

Fifteen

On Tuesdays, the only day no one had an after-school activity or meeting, the Vanderbeekers went to the cat café. It was nice to hang out in the warm café, spend time with the cats, and do homework with a pile of warm cookies fresh from the oven.

Jessie found herself still irritated by her earlier conversation with Isa and Allegra. Why hadn't Isa mentioned she was having some kind of issue with Benjamin before? Was it because Isa didn't think Jessie would understand?

Did Jessie not understand things? Was that why Orlando had never told her about his mom and their living situation? Jessie always told Isa and Orlando everything that was bothering her. She started to question why her two best friends were keeping things from her.

As Jessie, Isa, and Allegra approached the café, they were greeted by a sight never before seen on that block. Crowded in front of the cat café were dozens of dogs. Dogs that towered over the fire hydrants, dogs the size of squirrels, yippy dogs, and silent dogs. Some had curly fur and some had straight hair so long that it brushed the ground; some had long, pointy faces while others had square, squashed faces. A few wore bandanas tied jauntily around their necks, while others sported studded collars.

"What the heck?" Jessie asked.

As they drew nearer, they saw Orlando, Oliver, Hyacinth, and Laney staring from behind the safety of the café window.

"Are you all here for the dog-walking services?" Allegra asked the crowd.

"We're looking for some guy named Orlando," a man said, pulling out his cell phone. "The email said there's a highly experienced and responsible dog walker named Orlando."

Allegra pushed her way to the bakery window and gestured for Orlando to come out. His brow creased in confusion, but he made his way to the door, followed by Hyacinth, Oliver, and Laney.

"Folks, here he is!" Allegra announced when Orlando stepped out onto the sidewalk. "The best dog walker in New York City!"

Orlando was immediately mobbed by dog owners asking him his hours and rates. Hyacinth, Oliver, and Laney were shoved to the side in the rush.

"I'm sorry," Orlando said over the noise. "What's going on?"

"We're responding to the posters for dog-walking

services," said a woman with two chubby dachshunds. "I need someone responsible to walk Fluffy and Petunia four times a day while I'm at work, and since I was the first one here, I should get priority. But before I sign up, I need you to take my dogs on a test walk so I can see if you have what it takes. If they don't respect you, they'll start doing stuff they're not supposed to do."

"Like what?" Laney asked, intrigued.

"Eat trash, chase bicycles, roll around in puddle water." The woman put her hands on her knees and bent down to her dogs. Her voice rose two octaves. "Right, sweetie tum-tums? Right, honey buns? Aren't you my good girls?"

The dachshunds blinked at her, then heaved identical sighs and lay down on the sidewalk, putting their heads on their paws.

"Orlando is very good with all types of dogs," Allegra said. "Why don't we discuss his rates?"

"I think there's been a misunderstanding," Orlando interjected.

A man wearing basketball shorts, a Superman

T-shirt, and flip-flops pushed to the front. "I need someone to walk Frodo of the Shire"—he put his hand on the head of the enormous Great Dane sitting next to him—"around one o'clock every weekday. What do you charge for a sixty-minute walk?"

Orlando peered at the poster the man was holding, then over the heads of the dog owners to seek out Jessie, Isa, and Allegra.

"I had nothing to do with it," Jessie called, arms raised in innocence.

Allegra beamed at Orlando. "You're going to be rich!"

Orlando closed his eyes and took a deep breath. When he opened them again, he looked at the crowd and said, "I'm so sorry you all wasted your time. Your dogs look, uh, charming, but my schedule is full at the moment. We'll contact you if spots open up."

"How did your schedule fill so quickly?" Fluffy and Petunia's owner complained. "I took a half day off from work to be here!"

"I'm sorry you wasted your time," Orlando said again. "Good luck with your dog-walking needs."

The crowd grumbled, but when they realized that Orlando was serious and there was no chance of hiring him to walk their dogs, they eventually dispersed.

"What the heck?" Orlando hissed at Isa and Allegra, when the dog owners were out of earshot.

"We can explain," Isa said. "Let's go inside." She led the way, and the Vanderbeekers and Allegra dropped into seats around the biggest table. Orlando, however, crossed his arms and refused to sit down.

"Well," Isa began in a quiet voice, "we had this idea that you probably wanted to earn some money, so Allegra and I made posters advertising dog-walking services. We wanted to, uh, surprise you with clients."

"Isn't that something you should have *asked* me about?" Orlando interjected, biting out the words. He glared at Jessie.

"Why are you looking at me?" Jessie said.

"It sounded like a better idea a few days ago," Isa admitted. "We were just trying to help."

Orlando swung around and glared at Oliver. "And you!"

Oliver had been staring at the cookie counter, and

his head whipped around when Orlando said his name. "What did I do?"

"Did you send Coach Mendoza a video of me playing football? Because all of a sudden he's calling nonstop, and I'm getting all these emails with practice information and uniform requirements and game-day instructions."

Oliver beamed and pumped his fists. "That's awesome! I knew they would want you!"

"But I don't *want* to join the football team," Orlando said. "You can't sign me up without asking me!"

None of the Vanderbeekers was used to Orlando raising his voice. Laney pulled her turtleneck up so high it covered her eyes, and Hyacinth dropped under the café table and pulled Purl One into her lap for comfort.

A beat of silence followed.

"You love football," Oliver said. "I thought you would be happy."

"I'm not a charity case," Orlando said. "You don't need to pay for my phone or buy my food or get me a job. I can take care of myself."

"We don't think you're a charity case," Isa said quickly.

"We want you to stay with Miss Josie and Mr. Jeet forever," Laney said from behind her turtleneck. "They want to be your guardians."

"How do you know that?" Orlando asked.

Jessie raised a sheepish hand. "I told them. But in my defense, it was *before* you told me not to share it with anyone."

Orlando was furious, and his voice grew even louder. "Did it ever occur to any of you that I don't want your help? You Vanderbeekers have a serious problem with intervening. You think you know how to fix everything!" He pointed at Oliver. "You, setting up football tryouts when you know I'm doing another sport right now!"

Oliver looked down at his hands. "I'm sorry," he mumbled.

Orlando turned on Isa and Allegra. "And you two, setting up a dog-walking business without even asking me!"

"We were just trying to help," Isa said again in a small voice.

"I DON'T WANT YOUR HELP!" Orlando exploded.

Purl One jumped off Hyacinth's lap and fled to the back of the café. The eyes of every customer in the café turned toward them.

"Hey, guys, can you keep it down?" Jason called from behind the counter.

Their table descended into quiet before Orlando spoke again. "I wish you would—"

Orlando's phone interrupted his thought. "Ugh, if this is Coach Mendoza again . . ." He held the phone to his ear. "What? Oh, hey, Aunt Josie. Oh no! I'll be right there!"

The Vanderbeekers, alarmed at his panicked voice, stood up. "Is everything okay?" they asked.

Orlando shoved his phone in his pocket and grabbed his backpack. "It's Mr. Jeet. He just went to the hospital."

Sixteen

As they rushed to Harlem Hospital, Laney thought about the last time she had been there. It was when Mr. Jeet had had a stroke, and Laney had gotten into Very Big Trouble bringing Paganini there.

"Come on, Laney," Oliver said. "Hurry up!"

Even though her legs were tired and her chest was burning, she forced herself to keep going. Thankfully, the hospital was not far from the cat café. When they arrived, Mama was waiting for them in the lobby, and Laney launched herself right into her mom's arms.

"What's going on?" Isa asked as Orlando and her siblings clustered around Mama.

"What room is he in?" Orlando asked, breathless.

"Three-oh-two, but—" Mama said, and Orlando sprinted for the elevators before she could say anything else. Laney tried to follow him, but Mama held her back and put her arms around her.

"Give him some time alone," Mama said. "Jessie, in a few minutes, you go up to make sure he's okay."

"Mama, you're scaring me. What's going on?" Jessie asked, her eyes wide with fear.

Laney, who had run into Mama's arms without even seeing her face, looked up to find her mom's eyes were swollen and red.

"Kids, he's not doing well," Mama said.

"But he's been taking medicine, right, Mama?" Laney said. "And we've been bringing him really healthy food. So he'll get better."

"How long will he be in the hospital?" Isa asked.

Mama took a deep breath. "I think we need to prepare ourselves."

"Prepare ourselves for what?" Laney asked, looking around at her siblings. Jessie's face had lost color, and Isa looked as if she might faint. Oliver appeared as confused as she was, and Hyacinth had gone still.

When no one responded, Oliver spoke up.

"Prepare ourselves for what?" Oliver asked. "What's going on?"

Mama closed her eyes, and when she opened them again, Laney saw something she had never seen before. It was as if the light in her mom's eyes, which usually brightened up a room, had been flicked off.

"We need to prepare ourselves," Mama said, "because Mr. Jeet is dying."

❀ ❀ ❀

Jessie felt as if she were walking in a dream. She could hear Laney wailing and Oliver saying, "I don't believe you. He's going to be fine. He's going to be *fine*." Mama was comforting them, and Jessie wanted nothing more than to stay there, in the warmth of her mom's orbit. But she knew Orlando needed her right now, and she forced herself to put one foot in front of the other until she reached the elevator. She stepped inside, her sneakers squeaking on the speckled linoleum tile. She found herself alone, and she put both hands on the metal railing that lined the elevator, bowed her head, and took deep breaths. A few seconds later, the elevator doors opened, and she followed the signs for room 302.

The hallways echoed with machines humming, soft sneakers padding against the floors, and whispered conversations between people wearing light-green scrubs. Room 302 was down the hall from the nurses' station, and when she peeked in there were two beds separated by a curtain hanging from the ceiling in the middle of the room. Mr. Jeet was lying in the bed closest to the door, his eyes closed and machines surrounding him. Orlando, his back toward Jessie, was standing at his bedside, his tall body seemingly half its size with his shoulders hunched over Mr. Jeet's body. Miss Josie was on the other side, one hand gripping Mr. Jeet's hands and the other stroking his head.

A nurse bustled past Jessie, and Jessie moved back a few steps. For some reason, she felt that the dynamic in the room would change if she went inside.

"Hello," the nurse said to Miss Josie, examining Mr. Jeet's clipboard. "The doctor just told me that you have decided to provide Mr. Jeet hospice care at your home."

"Yes," Miss Josie said.

"We can make him quite comfortable in his last days here at the hospital," the nurse continued, not looking up from his clipboard.

"We think he will be most comfortable in his home, surrounded by family," Miss Josie replied.

The nurse nodded. "Of course. I have the discharge forms here. I understand that you already have a hospital bed in your home, as well as a nurse who can provide end-of-life care?"

"Yes," Miss Josie answered.

"I just need your signature here, and then I'll call for someone to help bring him home," the nurse said.

"Thank you," Miss Josie said, her voice cracking.

The nurse left the room, and Jessie made her way inside and stood next to Orlando. He didn't look at her, and she had a feeling he was barely holding it together. Jessie leaned into him, and Orlando rested his chin on the top of her head. A few minutes later, the rest of the Vanderbeekers trailed in with Papa and Mr. Beiderman. They were so quiet that Jessie didn't realize they were there until she felt Papa's arm around her waist.

And there they stood, forming a circle around one

of the greatest men they had ever known. And as they held hands and both gave and accepted comfort from one another, the ten people who loved Mr. Jeet the most each wondered how on earth they could possibly make it through one day without him.

WEDNESDAY, OCTOBER 23 TO FRIDAY, OCTOBER 25

Seventeen

Orlando and Miss Josie had not left the apartment since Tuesday night, when Mr. Jeet was discharged from the hospital. They stayed by his side, talking to him as if he were listening to every word. The Vanderbeekers spent every moment after school with him, canceling all their afternoon activities. Mama and Papa reduced their hours at work and spent the rest of the time caring for Miss Josie, making meals and cleaning her apartment and managing the nursing staff who were there on a rotating basis. Mr. Beiderman stopped by multiple times a day to read poetry to Mr. Jeet. The days passed in a blur, the moments captured in vignettes.

Wednesday, 12:38 p.m.

Mr. Beiderman sat in the armchair, midday light streaming through the lace curtains. His spectacles rested on the tip of his nose as he read from a book of poems by Joy Harjo.

Remember the sky that you were born under,
Know each of the star's stories.

In the kitchen, Ms. Fran stirred a small pot of broth on the stove. "Be at peace," she said in a quiet voice.

Wednesday, 5:06 p.m.

Laney arrived with Paganini and nestled the gray rabbit under Mr. Jeet's arm. She checked beneath the hospital bed and saw Billie Holiday lying there, her mournful eyes looking out. Laney flattened herself against the ground and wiggled her way close to Billie Holiday, then reached to scratch behind her ears. She scooted back out, stood up, and climbed onto the bed, her legs dangling off the side.

"Do you remember the first time I introduced you to Paganini?" she asked Mr. Jeet. "He was so little and cute, and you bought me a rabbit-ear headband so we could match. And remember when Paganini was a baby and he got lost in your apartment, and we looked everywhere for him? We finally found him sleeping in your boots!" Laney leaned over to look closely at Mr. Jeet's closed eyes. "Can you hear me, Mr. Jeet? Are you sleeping?"

Wednesday, 6:43 p.m.

"Can I tempt you to eat something?" Mama asked Miss Josie.

"It smells good," Miss Josie said, taking the small bowl of vegetable soup Mama offered her. She ate a few spoonfuls, then put it down on the side table next to her.

"Did I ever tell you how he proposed to me?" Miss Josie asked Mama.

The Vanderbeeker kids, who were sitting in various spots around the apartment, listened in.

"It was after work at the New York Botanical Garden, and we were taking a walk through the gardens at the end of the day like we always did. He suggested we head through the native forests, and we took a path that led to the Bronx River, where there was a pretty waterfall. There, on the stone bridge, was a whole line of our coworkers, all holding multicolored umbrellas, even though there wasn't a cloud in the sky. When I pointed it out to Mr. Jeet, he waved at our coworkers, and they all tilted the tops of the umbrellas toward us. There was a letter on the top of each umbrella, and all together they spelled out 'Will You Marry Me?'"

Wednesday, 8:17 p.m.

Night had fallen on the city, and only one lamp and a few candles were lit inside Miss Josie and Mr. Jeet's apartment. Orlando was standing by the hospital bed, his hand over Mr. Jeet's, while Mr. Beiderman sat in the armchair next to Orlando, reading from a book of poems by Li-Young Lee. Princess Cutie sat on Mr. Jeet's bed, her paws kneading the knit blanket that covered him.

> *There are days we live*
> *as if death were nowhere*
> *in the background; from joy*
> *to joy to joy, from wing to wing,*

from blossom to blossom to
impossible blossom, to sweet impossible blossom.

Thursday, 2:48 p.m.
"Why don't you play the violin?" Miss Josie suggested when she saw Isa.

Isa shook her head. She felt as if her body had been trembling for days. Her fingers were cold and stiff, and she wasn't sure she could find the notes. Instead, she put some of her favorite music on in the background—Niccolò Paganini's duet for guitar and violin—and let it wash over her.

Thursday, 3:06 p.m.
Hyacinth finished the hat she had been knitting for Mr. Jeet, weaving in and clipping the loose ends. She had made the hat out of thick navy-blue yarn, and Miss Josie helped lift his head so Hyacinth could put it on him.

"It fits him perfectly," Miss Josie told her. "It will keep him very warm."

Hyacinth nodded; then she headed into the bathroom so she could cry without anyone seeing her. She sat on the edge of the tub, scrubbing her eyes with tissue, and soon she heard Mr. Beiderman reading a poem by one of her favorite writers, Lucille Clifton.

> *may the tide*
> *that is entering even now*
> *the lip of our understanding*
> *carry you out*

Thursday, 4:08 p.m.

"Orlando and I both qualified for the robotics team at school," Jessie said to Mr. Jeet. She had no idea if he could hear her, and it felt weird to talk to him when he was so unresponsive. "Actually, there were a lot more applicants than spots, so it's sort of a big deal. We start next week, and our first competition is in December."

Jessie shuffled her feet, wondering why it didn't seem to bother Laney to talk to Mr. Jeet. Miss Josie put a hand on Jessie's shoulder.

"That sounds great, honey," she said. "I'm proud of you and Orlando. I know you'll do an excellent job."

Thursday, 7:54 p.m.

Billie Holiday had not budged from under the hospital bed since Tuesday night, refusing to come out even for meals. Three times a day, Orlando squeezed an arm underneath the bed so he could take her outside to go to the bathroom. Laney had tossed multiple treats under the bed, but Billie Holiday never ate them. When Princess Cutie made her daily visits with Mr. Beiderman, she beelined for the hospital bed and hunted down the treats. Billie Holiday would watch her with sad eyes, not lifting her head from the floor.

And Mr. Beiderman read, this time from the poet Langston Hughes.

I've known rivers:
Ancient, dusky rivers.

My soul has grown deep like the rivers.

Friday, 2:14 a.m.

Miss Josie stood up and stretched. Orlando had fallen asleep on the couch, one arm draped over his eyes.

The night nurse, a woman named Ms. Rudy, looked up from the dining room table, where she was doing a crossword puzzle.

"He seems like a nice man," Miss Rudy commented, looking at Mr. Jeet.

"He is the best person I have ever known," Miss Josie replied. "How much time do you think he has left?"

Miss Rudy stood up and checked his vitals. "It's always hard to say, but I think we're getting close."

Miss Josie nodded. Then she climbed up into the hospital bed with Mr. Jeet and held him close.

Friday, 4:36 a.m.

Miss Josie called Mama that Friday morning to ask the Vanderbeekers to come up to the second floor as soon as possible. She also requested that Isa please bring her violin. Ten minutes later, the Vanderbeekers knocked on the door. Mr. Beiderman was already there, the lines around his eyes looking particularly deep. They found Miss Josie standing in her usual spot next to Mr. Jeet's bed. Orlando was next to her, his back bowed in grief. Mr. Jeet was awake: for the first time in many days, the Vanderbeekers saw his eyes opened. Billie Holiday lay under the bed, her ears alert.

"You're awake!" Laney said to Mr. Jeet, taking his hand and giving it three squeezes, which meant "I love you."

"He's not doing well," Miss Josie said. "It's time to say goodbye."

"But he squeezed my hand back!" Laney said. "He's getting better!"

When Miss Josie looked back at Laney and shook her head, Laney burst into tears and buried her head in his chest. "Don't go, Mr. Jeet," she sobbed.

Wordlessly, Isa took out her violin and tuned it quietly. Then she placed her bow on the string and began one of Mr. Jeet's recent favorite pieces, "Casta Diva" from *Norma* by Vincenzo Bellini. As the rich notes echoed through the brownstone, the Vanderbeekers took turns saying the last things they wanted him to hear. Mama kissed his cheek and whispered in his ear. Then she gently pried Laney's hands from Mr. Jeet's arms and pulled Laney into a hug.

Papa took Mr. Jeet's hand in both of his. "Thank you for teaching my kids to be their truest, best selves."

Hyacinth leaned over the bed and hugged him, tears streaming from her eyes. "I love you more than all the stars in the universe," she said, her head nestled in the crook of his neck.

Oliver had no words; he just placed his hand over Mr. Jeet's heart and stood there until Papa put his hand on Oliver's shoulder and led him away so Jessie could say goodbye.

Jessie pressed a medal she had won at last year's science fair into his hand. "I'm going to be a scientist one day. I'll make you proud, I promise," she told him.

Orlando grabbed Mr. Jeet's hand. "Thank you for treating me like a son." Mr. Jeet blinked slowly, then squeezed Orlando's hand back.

The final words came from Miss Josie. "You've filled the last fifty-seven years of my life with laughter, friendship, and surprises. Your love has astounded me." She leaned down and kissed his cheek. "Now be at rest."

At 5:12 a.m. on Friday, October 25, as the final notes of "Casta Diva" lingered in the air, Mr. Jeet smiled and closed his eyes for the last time.

Eighteen

While Mama and Papa stayed with Miss Josie and Orlando to help with arrangements, the Vanderbeeker kids went back downstairs to get some rest. It was still dark outside, and when they opened the door, they found Franz, George Washington, and Tuxedo at the door. Franz woofed, Tuxedo meowed, and George Washington dashed to his food bowl. Hyacinth dropped to the ground and put her arms around Franz, weeping into his neck. Isa and Jessie put out food for the animals, and afterward, they all made their way to Isa and Jessie's bedroom.

Hyacinth could not stop crying. Laney went right for Isa's bed and buried herself under the covers, Tuxedo nuzzling his way in behind her. Hyacinth sat on

Isa's bed as well, grabbing Isa's stuffed wombat and holding it close to her stomach while occasionally wiping her eyes and nose with her sweatshirt sleeves. Franz jumped up on the bed and curled against Hyacinth's side, and Isa didn't protest even though she really didn't like it when Franz got her white comforter dirty.

"I can't believe he's gone," Oliver said, falling onto Jessie's messy bed and punching one of her pillows.

Isa's eyes were swollen and red as she nudged Hyacinth to the side and got into bed with her and Laney. "Nothing will ever be the same."

"He was doing fine," Laney said, her voice muffled by the blankets she had buried herself under. "He squeezed my hand."

"He's been sick for a long time," Jessie said. "A long, long time."

The Vanderbeekers fell silent. Then the sound of the front door opening and closing interrupted the quiet. Jessie walked to the window and looked out.

"It's Orlando," she said.

Hyacinth got up and joined Jessie at the window,

Franz following her. Orlando was going down the brownstone stairs to the sidewalk, his hands shoved into his pockets. A second later, the brownstone door opened again, and Mr. Beiderman emerged and hurried down the steps. He caught up with Orlando and put an arm around him. Then the two of them walked down 141st Street, and Hyacinth strained her neck to watch until they disappeared from sight.

"Mr. Beiderman will take care of him," Hyacinth said.

"He's going to leave us too," Jessie said to herself, but Hyacinth overheard.

"Who? Orlando?" Hyacinth asked, fresh tears filling her eyes.

Jessie, seeming only then to realize she had spoken out loud, looked at Hyacinth and went toward her bed without answering. "I'm going to sleep," she told Oliver, who was lying on her bed.

Oliver grunted, rolled off the bed, and headed out the door. A few seconds later, his bedroom door slammed. Jessie got into her bed and pulled the covers over her head.

Hyacinth was still by the window, and she slid to the ground. Franz was there to soften her landing, so she wrapped her arms around him, buried her face in his neck, and fell asleep.

✦ ✦ ✦

It was late morning by the time Oliver woke up. The sun was shining through his tiny window, and birds were chirping. He could hear Miss Josie walking above him, her steady, firm footfalls. He listened for Mr. Jeet's footsteps next: lighter, with a slight shuffle. When he didn't hear them, he thought that Mr. Jeet was probably resting. And then he remembered: he would never hear Mr. Jeet's footsteps again.

Oliver rolled over and buried his head under his pillow to block out the light of the day. His eyes burned, but no tears came. A few moments later, his door opened. Maybe if he stayed buried under the covers, whoever it was would leave.

"Hey, Oliver," came Mama's voice.

Oliver grunted.

"I just wanted to see how you're doing." The scent

of something familiar wafted through the room, made its way under the covers, and entered his nose. "I brought cookies," she said.

But cookies held no appeal. He wasn't hungry; he just wanted to sleep and sleep and forget that there was a world without Mr. Jeet in it.

"I'm here if you want to talk," Mama said, laying a hand on the blanket where his head was. "I'll leave the cookies on your desk. Here's your water bottle in case you're thirsty."

He felt a slight pressure next to him; then he heard the door close. He sat up and opened his water bottle and took a long drink, but the thought of getting out of bed for the cookies made him nauseous. Then the tears came back, as if a well had been replenished. He cried until he fell back asleep.

❋ ❋ ❋

Isa woke up to the smell of cookies and macaroni and cheese. Macaroni and cheese was her comfort food, so she rubbed her eyes and forced herself to sit up. Early-afternoon sunshine poured through the windows. Isa's twin sister was still asleep, a Jessie-sized lump under a pile of blankets. Laney was nowhere to be seen. Hyacinth lay on the floor with Franz; someone had put a pillow under her head and a thick knit blanket over her body.

When Isa got out of bed, Franz opened his eyes and his tail thumped against the floor. He didn't budge from his spot next to Hyacinth. Isa leaned down and scratched his ears.

"Good dog," she said to him. "Take care of Hyacinth, will you?"

Isa put a hoodie on over her shirt and headed down to the kitchen. Even though she had slept for several hours, she felt exhausted. Her hair was dirty and her pajamas were wrinkled. When she got downstairs, she saw Mama at the stove and Laney next to her, standing on a footstool. The familiar sight gave Isa a tiny bit of comfort.

"Hey, honey," Mama said, kissing Isa's temple. "How are you doing?"

"I'm sad," Laney interjected. "Mama said macaroni and cheese would make me feel better, but I'm not sure that's true."

"Did I hear 'macaroni and cheese'?" Papa asked as he came down the stairs, freshly showered, his hair wet. He kissed Mama's cheek and then peeked at the several pots on the stove. "Are these collards? Be still, my heart."

"Thinking of Mr. Jeet made me think of his favorite foods," Mama said. "He did love his Southern food."

"This makes me miss him more," Isa said, looking gloomily at the pots.

"It makes me sad, too," Mama said, "but it also makes me happy thinking about him. He used to sit right there at our table and tuck into the mac and cheese, fried chicken, and collards like he had never eaten before in his life."

"Remember when you finally fixed cornbread exactly the way he liked it?" Isa said. "I thought he was going to do a dance right there on top of the dinner table."

"Took me two years to get that recipe just right for him," Mama said.

There was a moment of contented silence as they thought about Mr. Jeet.

Isa coughed. "Will there be, you know, a funeral for him?"

"Yes, we've been talking to the church about it," Papa said. "It will probably be on Monday. Mama will help Miss Josie notify friends and family tomorrow. Which reminds me, I have to arrange for that company to pick up the hospital bed later today."

"He didn't even have it for a week," Isa said. "And we raised so much money for it too."

"It's okay," Mama said. "It was a rental, so the extra money we raised will go toward the funeral costs, which will be really helpful for Miss Josie."

"I don't want to go to the funeral," Laney said as she started to cry again. "It's just going to make me really sad."

Papa gathered her in his arms. "I know, honey. But do you know what? All of these feelings we're having are so strong because we loved him so much. And that says a lot about how amazing he was."

"I wish I could talk to him again," Laney said, tears spilling. "I have so many things to tell him."

"Me too," said Isa and Mama, moving to join Laney and Papa in their hug.

Nineteen

It was nearly four o'clock when the Vanderbeeker kids found themselves all together again. Oliver had gone outside to feed the chickens and hadn't returned after twenty minutes, so Hyacinth went outside to check on him. When Franz woke up from his nap to find that Hyacinth wasn't there, he barked at the back door until Isa opened it to let him out. Isa noticed Oliver and Hyacinth sitting in the treehouse, their legs dangling off the balcony, so she stepped outside, dodged the chickens that wove around her feet, and climbed up the ladder. Laney and Jessie, who were wandering around the brownstone with no purpose, heard the back door close. They went outside to see what everyone was doing, then scaled the ladder, too.

"Grab the candy, will you?" Oliver asked when he saw Jessie.

Jessie lifted the lid to the storage chest and opened the false bottom where Oliver kept his rapidly dwindling candy supply. She grabbed the last bags of Sour Patch Kids and jelly beans, then joined her siblings.

A few minutes later, the five kids were sitting in a line on the balcony, passing the bags of candy back and forth. They were all grateful that the balcony faced north so they could avoid looking in the direction of Mr. Jeet and Miss Josie's place. Franz sat directly beneath Hyacinth just in case she fell out of the treehouse. The chickens circled him, pecking at the grass around his feet.

"This is the worst day in the world," Laney said as she took a handful of jelly beans. She sorted through them, taking out all the orange ones and handing them to Oliver. He wordlessly crammed them into his mouth.

"My head hurts," Isa said, rubbing her temples.

"You're probably dehydrated," Jessie noted. "Drink some water."

"Okay," Isa said, then ate another Sour Patch Kid.

"Mama said the funeral is on Monday," Laney said. "What will happen at the funeral?"

"Well," Isa said, "people who knew and loved him will gather at the church. Some people will speak. Triple J might give a sermon."

"That's it?" Laney said. "It sounds so sad."

"It *is* sad," Oliver said. "It's a funeral."

Laney squished her face at him. "I thought it would be different."

Oliver scoffed. "What, you thought it was like a party or something?"

"Sort of," Laney said. "I don't want to go to a funeral and be even *more* sad. I don't think Mr. Jeet would want that."

"You have to go to the funeral," Oliver said. "Otherwise people will think you didn't love him."

"Of course I loved him!" Laney said. "I just don't want to be there, thinking about how he's not here with me anymore." She rubbed her eyes hard.

"I understand why you don't want to go," Isa said. "But it's a way to support Miss Josie and Orlando. Plus, Mama and Papa are helping with the arrangements."

"Laney, I think what you're saying makes sense," Jessie said.

"Really?" Laney asked. Jessie almost never understood her.

"I don't think Mr. Jeet would want us to go to his funeral and mope around."

"But Mama and Papa and Miss Josie have already planned it and everything," Isa said.

"True, but maybe we can do something afterward, in the garden," Jessie said.

"We can have a party!" Laney said. "And we can play jazz music because he loved jazz, and we can all garden, and we can make his favorite foods and his favorite cookies!"

"We should ask Miss Josie first," Isa said cautiously. "Maybe she won't want to have such a big thing after the funeral."

"I'll text her," Jessie said. She typed out a message while Laney looked over her shoulder and made suggestions, and then she pressed send. "She's probably not by her phone," Jessie warned Laney. "She might not answer—"

Jessie's phone pinged.

"It that her?" Laney asked.

"Wow, she's fast," Jessie said. "She thinks it's a great idea and we should go ahead and plan it."

Laney smiled, and she realized that she hadn't smiled in a long time. Her mouth felt weird making that shape, but it felt good, too. Back when Mr. Jeet was speaking, he did so much to make her smile, like training Paganini to do tricks or making funny hats with newspaper.

Laney took another jelly bean and chewed on it, thinking of all the things that Mr. Jeet would love at his garden party.

"I think we should hang Hyacinth's yarn garlands in the trees," Laney said. "It would make it really pretty."

"I can help hang them," Oliver volunteered.

Laney shook her head. "I'm going to ask Orlando since he's so tall. He probably doesn't need a ladder."

"He's not that much taller than I am," Oliver grumbled.

"True," Jessie said, "if you don't consider two feet that much of a difference."

"Two feet!" Oliver exclaimed. "Not even close!"

"Have you heard from Orlando?" Hyacinth asked Jessie.

Jessie nodded. "He texted me a few times. I think he's doing okay. It was weird—this morning I got the feeling that he's going to go back to Georgia after the marathon."

Isa looked at her. "Really? Why?"

Jessie chewed on another jelly bean. "With Mr. Jeet gone, he'll probably want Miss Josie to take her bedroom back. And then where would he sleep?"

"In the living room?" Laney suggested.

"I don't think that would work for the long term," Jessie said.

"Ooh, I have a great idea!" Laney said. "He can move in with us!" She looked around for affirmation. Her siblings crunched their candy in silence.

"We have no room," Oliver said. "He barely even fits in my room."

It was true. Oliver's room was a walk-in closet that they'd converted into a bedroom for him.

"He can take our room," Hyacinth suggested, "and Laney and I can move in with Mama and Papa!"

"I get to be on Mama's side," Laney said at once. "Papa snores too loud."

"I'm one hundred percent positive that Mama and Papa would not want to share a bedroom with you two," Oliver said. "No, wait. *One thousand* percent positive."

"I think it's more complicated than just having a room for him," Jessie said. "I've been doing some research, and we can't just take him in. We're not technically his family. If we want him to live with us, we would have to apply for custody and go to court. And anyway, we don't know whether he'll stay here or go back to Georgia. But he does need a legal guardian soon."

"We need to be sensitive," Isa said. "He got mad at us for barging ahead and trying to make everything in his life perfect without involving him in any of our decisions. We definitely screwed up."

"So what can we do?" Oliver asked.

"I think," Hyacinth said in her quiet, wise way, "we need to love him like Mr. Jeet loved him. He always made Orlando know that he was on his side."

Isa hooked an arm around Hyacinth. "Love the way Mr. Jeet did? I think that's a perfect way to honor him."

A breeze touched their faces and rustled the leaves around them, and for a second the sun peeked through the clouds and a beam of light hit the golden leaves and made the air shimmer. It was a tiny moment of hope that Mr. Jeet was somehow still with them, surrounding them with his love.

MONDAY, OCTOBER 28

Six Days Until the New York City Marathon

Twenty

The Vanderbeekers had spent the weekend planning the garden party and helping Miss Josie as she received visitors who wanted to express their condolences. The Vanderbeekers put themselves in charge of greeting guests, Oliver taking their coats and Isa receiving the lasagnas and casseroles the visitors inevitably brought. By Monday, every freezer in the brownstone was packed full of what the residents had dubbed Condolence Casserole, and Hyacinth believed that they now had enough to last until Christmas.

On Monday morning, they woke early to a crisp autumn day with a clear blue sky. Mama had set out bagels and fruit, but no one had much of an appetite except Tuxedo, who kept leaping on top of the table so he could steal licks of cream cheese. The Vanderbeeker kids spent a couple of hours making final preparations for the garden party. At nine thirty, they made their way to the church. To Hyacinth's surprise, 141st Street was clogged with traffic.

"What are all of these cars doing here?" Laney asked Mama as they walked hand in hand down the street.

"I think they're filled with people who want to pay their respects to Mr. Jeet," Mama said.

But as they neared the church, they realized that not only was the long line of cars for Mr. Jeet, there was also a long line of *people* wrapped around the corner and spilling over onto Frederick Douglass Boulevard.

"Wow!" Laney said. "Mama, you did a *really* good job letting people know about the funeral."

"He had a lot of friends," Mama said. "I realized that when I started going through Miss Josie's address book. We've only known him for the past ten years, when he was more solitary. But he's had a very full life. I wish I could ask him more about it now."

"We can ask *them*," Laney said, gesturing around at the line.

Hyacinth looked closer at the line, which included people of all ages, heights, hairstyles, and footwear. She recognized some of them, who turned to her and smiled, but most were complete strangers.

"How could Mr. Jeet have so many friends I never met?" Laney asked. "I thought best friends were supposed to know everything about each other."

Mama smiled. "I'm sure there's plenty Mr. Jeet didn't know about you, Laney. There are things I don't know about you, and I'm your mom! Mr. Jeet lived a long time, nearly seventy years more than you have. He's made a lot of friends."

Hyacinth looked out at the line of people entering the church, and a wave of sadness fell over her at the thought of not knowing much about Mr. Jeet. So much of their time together had been spent with Hyacinth telling Mr. Jeet about her day or answering his questions. Later, after his strokes, there'd been less talking and more just sitting together in a contented silence. She wished she could turn back time and ask him to tell her more stories about his life. Seeing all the unfamiliar faces made her feel farther away from him than ever.

Since Mama and Papa were involved in organizing the funeral, the Vanderbeekers could enter through the service door at the back of the church, which meant they didn't have to get in line. They found Miss Josie at the front of the church, shaking hand after hand and responding to person after person coming up to her saying, "I'm sorry" or "We'll miss him" or "He lived a good life." Not too long after that, people were seated and the service began. The Vanderbeekers were asked to sit in the front row with Miss Josie and Orlando, but Hyacinth wished she were in the back. She felt hundreds of eyes staring at the back of her head.

A big photograph of Mr. Jeet was on an easel just a few feet away from them, so Hyacinth had plenty of time during the service to stare at every detail. The photo must have been taken before she had known him. He was impeccably dressed in a white button-down with thin gray stripes and a jaunty peacock-blue bow tie, but his face was smoother and he didn't have as many eye crinkles.

The service was long, with a lot of talking, and she was glad for the times the gospel choir stood and sang, their beautiful burgundy robes swirling around their ankles. Their rich voices soared through the church, bouncing off the domed ceiling. They sang "Amazing Grace," followed by "Trouble of This World." Finally, when the service was about to end, they finished with a song called "I Wanna Be Ready" that Hyacinth remembered hearing in a video her teacher had shown at school. It was a performance by a dance company started by a man named Alvin Ailey. They had a piece called *Revelations* that was the most beautiful thing Hyacinth had ever seen.

Before the service ended, Triple J announced that a garden party in honor of Mr. Jeet would follow next door and everyone was invited to join his family and friends as they celebrated his life.

Over the weekend, the Vanderbeekers had gone around to local businesses to let them know about the funeral and garden celebration. They had seen many of the people who worked in their neighborhood in the service, but when they walked next door to the garden to help Mama put out cookies, they were surprised to see that many of the people who worked at the local restaurants had also brought food. There was so much that Oliver and Orlando and Angie and Jessie returned to the church to lug more tables into the garden. Isa, Mama, Hyacinth, and Laney sorted through the food and set it out on big platters from the church kitchen. There were dozens of cheese croissants and apple turnovers from Castleman's Bakery, boxes upon boxes of fried chicken from Kennedy's Fried Chicken, a mountain of biscuits and strawberry butter from a local breakfast place, and pots of coffee and hot water for tea from Harlem Coffee.

After the food was set up, Jessie pulled out Miss Josie's turntable and Orlando connected it to large speakers, and Jessie put on Mr. Jeet's favorite Ella Fitzgerald record. The Vanderbeekers sat behind a table with a big sign that said "Share a Memory." They had cut thick strips of fabric in a rainbow of colors and put out cups filled with fabric markers. People were asked to write one sentence of their favorite Mr. Jeet memories on the fabric and tie it on the chainlink fence at the entrance to the garden.

Hyacinth felt shy at the thought of talking to hundreds of strangers, but as people came to the table and asked about the project, she saw their smiling faces and remembered that they were all connected because of Mr. Jeet. Once she explained the project, people were eager to write their memories down. Afterward, they would tell the longer versions to the Vanderbeekers.

"Are you the Vanderbeekers?" a woman asked when she and her husband stopped by the table.

"We are," Laney said, her chest puffing out.

"Oh, we've heard so much about you!" the woman said, then looked at her husband. "These are the kids that Mr. Jeet talked about all the time." She turned back to the kids. "My father grew up with him in Georgia, and whenever Mr. Jeet came to visit, he would show us photos and tell stories about your family. He was like a proud grandfather."

"Is your dad here?" Laney asked, looking around at the packed garden.

"My father passed away a few years ago," the woman told them. "But he had a long and wonderful career in the Georgia state senate." She went on to talk about how her father and Mr. Jeet had gone to college together at Savannah State University and had been involved with a group who wanted to bring attention to the lack of voting rights in Alabama.

And that is how the Vanderbeekers learned something entirely new about Mr. Jeet. When he'd been in college, he was one of the hundreds of people who, when marching from Selma to Montgomery for voting rights, were brutally confronted by state and local lawmen on the Edmund Pettus Bridge in Selma on March 7, 1965.

"Did Mr. Jeet get hurt?" Oliver asked, his eyes wide with this new revelation of Mr. Jeet as a young man.

"No, he and my dad were at the back of the march and were able to get off the bridge quickly," she said. "I have a photo of them from college. Hold on." She took out her phone and scrolled through the photos. "Ah, here it is." She passed the phone to the Vanderbeekers and they huddled around it, staring at a black-and-white photo of a young, dapper version of Mr. Jeet, his spine straight and his eyes sparkling. Even back then, he wore a bow tie. He stood with his friend, their arms slung around each other's shoulders, the logo of Savannah State College looming behind them.

"He adored you all," she said to the Vanderbeekers before she and her husband went off to tie their fabric pieces to the chainlink fence. "You gave him so much joy and kept him young."

Buoyed by this encounter, the Vanderbeekers greeted the next people who visited the table. They were gardeners Mr. Jeet had worked with at the New York Botanical Garden.

"Oh, I remember you! You're the Vanderbeekers!" everyone said when they introduced themselves. "We remember you from his retirement party. Of course, there were only three of you back then," they said while looking at the three older kids.

"He spoke of you like you were his grandkids," one of them said. "He showed us photos of you all the time."

The Vanderbeekers soaked up the stories of Mr. Jeet, and then the gardeners wrote their memories on strips of fabric. "His hands were like magic with the plants" and "He loved the garden" and "He treasured every living thing." Then they complimented the Vanderbeekers on their work on the community garden, admired the lavender maze, which played classical music when people walked through it, and gave Jessie and Orlando advice on irrigation and how to create the perfect environment for making compost. Laney and Hyacinth had lots of questions about tomatoes; they had tried growing them that summer and ended up with huge tangles of vines and bugs and no tomatoes at all. The gardeners shared their best tomato tips (of which there were a lot, sometimes contradictory, which set off a debate about pruning and whether the addition of an Epsom-salt blend while watering made a difference or not).

After that, they met people who had lived in the neighborhood back when Papa was growing up and had since moved out of the city. They shared memories about how Mr. Jeet would sit outside on the brownstone stoop in the evenings and chat with people coming home from work. He would take post-dinner walks in the summer, occasionally joining a group of teens for a game of basketball or helping a family carry furniture up the stairs to their new apartment. People called him the mayor of 141st Street.

Eventually the emotions that Hyacinth had harbored during the beginning of the funeral began to change. Instead of feeling as if she didn't really know Mr. Jeet, she realized that he had always been the same person she'd known him to be, even though he had lived a whole lifetime before she was even born. And that knowledge filled a little of that lonely place in her heart that had been missing him so desperately.

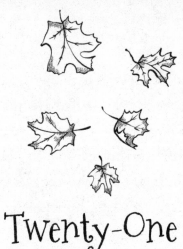

Twenty-One

Jessie was pulled away from the memory table to help Mama with the food, and as she loaded more fried chicken onto a platter, she caught sight of Orlando surrounded by a group of people she had never met. Curious but not wanting to interrupt, she strolled past the group in hopes of overhearing their conversation.

"We miss you," said a woman who looked very much like Miss Josie.

"The football team stinks without you," said a boy who looked about their age.

"It's so cold here," a woman wearing bold purple glasses commented, pulling her jacket closer around her. "It was seventy-two degrees when we left Georgia."

"When your mom comes back," another lady said, "you know she'll be in Georgia. She never did like the big city."

"Why'd you leave, anyway?" the boy asked. "You had a good job at the farm stand, you were all set to play quarterback, and you know Grandma makes the best Southern food in the county. Honestly, I can't see you staying here. It's so . . . dirty. And crowded."

"I like it here," Orlando said. "It doesn't seem dirty to me."

But Jessie noticed that his voice didn't have much energy behind it. Did he seem resigned? Jessie wondered if part of it was the grief of still not hearing from his mom or because Mr. Jeet was gone. Either way, she felt as if her best friend was slipping away and there was nothing she could do about it.

She got ready to keep moving past Orlando and his Georgia fan club—Mama still needed help with the food—but Orlando caught sight of her and called out her name. She made her way to him, lifting her hand in an awkward wave.

"Who are you?" asked the teen, squinting at her suspiciously.

"Who are *you?*" Jessie shot back, already annoyed by him.

"This is Jessie Vanderbeeker," Orlando explained, and everyone in the group said "Ahhh" in a way that let her know this was not the first time they had heard her name.

"You live in the brownstone," the teen said knowledgeably. "You're the science nerd."

Orlando quickly interjected, "I think we prefer the term 'science expert.'"

Jessie was unbothered by the comment. She *was* a science nerd; who cared?

"We've heard so much about you," said the woman who looked like Miss Josie. "I'm Miss Josie's sister, Orlando's other great-aunt. You can call me Aunt Jolene."

"Nice to meet you, Aunt Jolene," Jessie said, holding out her hand.

"Nice to meet you as well," she said, smiling.

Miss Josie came by the group, kissing everyone on the cheek and getting her freshly applied lipstick on them. The teen rubbed it off vigorously.

"Orlando, would you grab me a cup of water, please?" Miss Josie asked.

"I'll go with you," Jessie said hurriedly.

"Me too," said the teen.

Jessie sighed; she really didn't like that guy and was hoping for some time with Orlando without crowds of people.

"I'm Jackson," the boy said as they made their way to the drinks table. "I'm Orlando's best friend."

Jessie wanted to clarify that *she* was Orlando's best friend and had been for years, but before she could say a word, Orlando bumped her elbow.

"Are you hungry?" he asked her before turning to Jackson. "This fried chicken is so good."

Jackson plucked a piece off the platter and took a bite. "It's okay. Can't compare to Aunt Jolene's cooking, that's for sure."

"That's for sure," Orlando agreed, but he took another bite of the chicken anyway. He didn't seem bothered by the subpar-chicken-that-was-not-made-by-Aunt-Jolene.

"Jessie's mom owns the local cookie café," Orlando

said to Jackson. "Best cookies ever. It got written up in a bunch of magazines. There's a table full of her cookies over there." Orlando pointed to the table, which was covered by a blue floral tablecloth.

Jackson eyed Jessie, then looked away. "Yeah, I'm not that hungry. Hey, so when are you coming back to Georgia? We sure could use your throwing arm. Team's not the same without you."

Orlando shook his head. "I haven't decided what I'm going to do yet."

Jessie breathed a sigh of relief, but Jackson continued to probe.

"What do you mean, you haven't decided? You want to stay *here?* The land of no football? No decent fried chicken?"

"This is a very nice neighborhood, thank you very much," Jessie said, glaring at Jackson. "Orlando is on the cross-country team, *and* he's going to help Mr. Beiderman run the New York City Marathon."

"Cross-country?" Jackson scoffed. "Now, *that* just sounds boring. Where's the strategy? Where's the teamwork?"

"There's strategy and teamwork," Orlando said.

"I'd like to see you run as far and as fast as Orlando can run," Jessie said. "Cross-country is really hard."

Jackson shook his head as if questioning whether Orlando was even worth knowing anymore.

"You need to come home," Jackson said. "Everyone misses you."

"I miss being down there too," Orlando said. "Like I said, I'm still thinking about it."

Jessie wanted to put in a good word about Harlem. But when she thought about what Orlando had told her about Georgia, about the huge football fields with perfectly trimmed grass and the big sky that surrounded them, she wondered how the little patch of grass that they called a garden could even compare. It must seem so puny and claustrophobic. And their skinny brownstone, where Orlando didn't even have his own bedroom? Jessie wouldn't blame him for choosing Georgia and football and his relatives over loud, polluted, crowded New York City.

And that left Jessie with more of an ache in her heart. Her time with Orlando was coming to an end.

By the time they'd gotten Miss Josie her water, the party was winding down. People were heading back to their cars or to the subway or bus, and Jessie stepped outside the garden to take a breath. The thought of losing yet another person she loved was too overwhelming to bear. She wrapped her arms around her stomach and wished she could visit Mr. Jeet just like she had done thousands of times in the past decade. Mr. Jeet always knew how to make her feel better when she was having a bad day.

An unexpected wind whipped down 141st Street, and Jessie pulled her jacket closer around her and zipped it up. A rustling noise made her pause; it wasn't the usual sound of cars rolling over autumn leaves down the street. She turned her head and found the source: it was the sound of hundreds of fabric strips snapping in the wind.

The fabric rippled like river rapids, but she still could see words here and there. Words like "laughter" and "warm" and "strong" and "curious." And she stood there, watching the fence and all those Mr. Jeet memories, the wind and the words washing over her, whispering over and over that everything would be okay.

Tuesday, October 29

Five Days Until the New York City Marathon

Twenty-Two

Mama and Papa had given the kids a choice about going to school the day after the funeral. Surprisingly, everyone decided to go. They had been absent since the previous Thursday, and they couldn't imagine just sitting in the brownstone thinking about how one person was missing.

It was one of those mornings when everything felt heavy, as if it took twice as much energy as usual to move. Clouds were so thick and gray that they seemed to weigh down the city with gloom. The Vanderbeekers dragged themselves out of bed and through the familiar routine of making their beds, brushing their teeth, changing, and sitting down for breakfast.

"The offer stands; you can stay home an extra day." Mama looked at her kids in concern.

"I think that's a good idea," Papa said. "We can play board games!"

"Ugh," Oliver responded. It was the first sound he had made since waking up.

"I'm not going to take that personally," Papa said.

"You shouldn't," Mama said, patting his shoulder. "Although it wouldn't hurt if you let the kids win at Bananagrams once in a while."

"Seriously," Jessie muttered under her breath. "So competitive."

Oliver stood up. "I've got to go. Coach Mendoza is having early basketball practice."

"I missed a test and two quizzes yesterday," Jessie said. "I'm going to get more behind if I stay home."

The kids gathered up their things and headed out the door. A fierce wind dipped in and slammed the door shut behind them, and the brownstone gave a sigh as they disappeared down the street.

✦ ✦ ✦

Hyacinth was so sad about Mr. Jeet that she didn't

even think about having to go in early and wait in the cafeteria. She had brought her knitting; it always helped to keep her hands busy. She had started a blanket for Orlando, and with the weather getting colder, she wanted to get it done quickly. She hoped to finish it by the marathon.

Without even bothering to see who was also at the third-grade table, Hyacinth sat down and pulled her knitting bag from her backpack. Her plan was to make a patchwork of squares in various colors that she would then sew together so it would end up looking like a quilt. She liked the idea of a quilt; her mom had made her a baby quilt when she was born that Hyacinth still slept with, despite the frayed edges and the batting having mostly disappeared after hundreds of washings. Quilts always made a place feel like home.

Hyacinth had calculated how many squares she'd need before she started to knit. She needed seventy total and had completed eighteen so far, and Herman had pitched in and made ten. Each square was eight by eight inches, and she'd determined that she needed seven squares across and ten squares down so it would be big enough for Orlando, who was six feet tall. That left forty-two squares to complete. Herman would help, but he had a lot more homework in sixth grade and less time for knitting these days.

She was in the middle of knitting a violet square, concentrating on making nice, even stitches, when she felt someone sit down next to her.

"What are you doing?"

Hyacinth glanced up briefly, positive that the question could not have been directed at her. There was Maria, looking right at her. Hyacinth looked behind her, then back at Maria.

"Me?" Hyacinth asked.

"This is knitting, right?" Maria asked, touching the square Hyacinth was working on.

"Yes," Hyacinth replied.

"Cool," Maria said, taking a bite of her french toast stick. "My grandma tried to teach me to knit once, but it was hard."

"Once you get the hang of it," Hyacinth said, "it's pretty easy."

"Can you show me? I'll trade you a french toast stick."

"Okay," Hyacinth said, opening up her bag of yarn, pushing it toward Maria, and taking the french toast stick in return. While Hyacinth ate, Maria combed through the bag and selected a light-blue yarn.

"Can I use this?" Maria asked.

"Sure." Hyacinth pulled out an extra pair of knitting needles and helped Maria cast on a row of twenty stitches, then showed her how to manipulate the needles and wrap the yarn to create a stitch. Maria tried it.

"I think I did it!" Maria said, triumphant. "Is this right?"

"That's perfect! Now you just need to do that over and over again a gazillion times, and then you get a blanket," Hyacinth said, returning to her violet knitting patch.

"Cool," Maria said. "Is this blanket for you?"

"No, it's for Orlando. I want to give him something for his room."

"What did you say about Orlando?" asked Leo, who had sat across from them, munching on a bowl of cereal.

"She's making a blanket for him," Maria said importantly. "I'm helping."

"I want to help," Leo said, abandoning his breakfast. "Can you teach me?"

Hyacinth looked up, startled. Leo had never, ever said anything to her before. "Um, sure." She dug out another set of knitting needles, and he came around the table so he could see what she was doing. When she thought he had the hang of it, he chose a red yarn and started to knit. As more third graders arrived, they gathered around the knitters to see what they were doing. Pretty soon, Hyacinth had given out all six pairs of her knitting needles, and there was a little group around her asking questions about whether they had made a mistake or whether there were other ways to knit than just the way she had shown them. As they got into a rhythm, they started planning how they could work on their squares at recess or after school.

"How come you eat breakfast here in the mornings?" Hyacinth asked Maria when the conversation turned to a video game that Hyacinth knew nothing about.

"My parents like it when I eat breakfast here," Maria told Hyacinth. "They both leave really early for work. My dad has to be at his construction site at seven, and my mom cleans apartments all the way in Brooklyn and it takes over an hour to get there on the subway."

"Do you like the food here?" Hyacinth asked as she got to the end of her knitting row and turned it around.

"It's okay," Maria said. "All the breakfast food here is so sweet, isn't it? In Ecuador, we would eat an empanada or a piece of bread with jam. Sometimes we would have plantains. Never french toast sticks."

"The breakfasts at my home are different from what they serve here too," Hyacinth said. "My mom sometimes makes us oatmeal with fruit, or blueberry pancakes, or breakfast cookies filled with oats and cranberries."

"You have *cookies* for *breakfast*?" Maria asked, her eyes wide.

"They're breakfast cookies," Hyacinth explained. "She makes them with honey or maple sugar instead of regular sugar. I'll bring you one next time if you want."

"I definitely want to try that," Maria said as she started a new row of stitches. "I'm getting tired of french toast sticks!"

When the bell rang, the sound surprised Hyacinth. She usually counted the seconds before the bell, setting her watch exactly to the school clocks so she would know how much time she had left. But today, for the first time, she wasn't waiting for the bell. Today, she wouldn't have minded hanging out in the cafeteria a little longer.

Twenty-Three

Isa was ambivalent about being back at school; she was glad for the distraction but not sure she was ready to face crowded hallways and demanding course work. When she opened her locker, a note fluttered to the floor.

> *I'm sorry about Mr. Jeet. What can I do to make you feel better? Makeovers at lunch? Lmk.*
> *Love,*
> *Allegra*

Isa smiled. She folded the note into her pocket, then went through the contents of her locker, taking out the books she needed for the morning.

She jumped when she felt a tap on her shoulder. Benny was standing there, a backpack slung over one shoulder.

"Hey, I'm sorry about Mr. Jeet," he said. "I tried to find you at the funeral, but it was so crowded."

"It's okay," Isa said. "The funeral was a little overwhelming with all those people."

Benny shifted to his other foot. "How was the garden party? I had a shift at the bakery, so I couldn't stay. A couple of customers told me about the memory fence. That's a good idea."

"I wasn't sure how it was going to turn out, but everyone seemed to really like it. When we were helping people, we met a lot of his old friends, and we learned things about his life that we never knew before—"

"Benjamin, I've been *waiting* for you," a girl interrupted, pulling on his backpack. Her eyebrows were sharp arrows on her face as she glared at Isa, then back at Benny. "You said we could talk about homecoming on the way to class." She spun around, her shiny hair swishing, and stomped down the hallway.

"Gotta go," Benny said, flashing a smile at Isa. "I'll catch up with you later." He jogged after the girl, and together they rounded the corner and disappeared from sight.

Isa watched them leave. She had been prepared to take Orlando's advice and ask Benny about homecoming, but it looked as if her question was answered: he was going to the dance with this girl.

Isa let out a breath and closed her locker, then set off down the hall toward her first class. As she jostled her way between the other students, she wondered why her heart felt so hollow. Benny was allowed to be friends with whoever he wanted to be friends with; it didn't matter to her, right?

The day passed in a blur. She saw Benny in biology, and he seemed perfectly normal the entire time. They did not talk about homecoming. At lunch she managed to avoid getting a makeover. Allegra, concerned at how tired Isa looked, met her after school and forced her to go to the cat café so they could get hot chocolate and catch up on the work she had missed when she was out of school. There was a line when they got there, so they put their bags down at their favorite table before getting in the queue.

"I saw Benjamin at the funeral yesterday," Allegra said as they inched up to the register. "He was wearing a suit. And *dress shoes*."

"Really?" Isa said, raising her eyebrows. Benny usually wore a sports jersey and jeans. She had seen him in a suit only a few times before, and always at school dances, but he definitely did *not* wear dress shoes for the dances.

"He looked pretty good," Allegra said. "Maybe he'll dress up for homecoming, too."

"I . . . don't think we're going to homecoming together," Isa said. "He's going with someone else."

Allegra leaned back and put her hands on her hips. "What?"

"Remember the girl I saw him with the other day? She was at school this morning," Isa said. "And they were talking about homecoming *and* he walked her to class."

"But—why—That's just—I can't—What?" Allegra was uncharacteristically short of words.

"It's fine," Isa assured her. "You know what? Let's just go to homecoming together. No guys."

Allegra got her words back. "I meant to tell you that yesterday in English Lit, Javier asked me to go with him. I was hoping for you-know-who"—she tilted her head toward Jason, who was filling cookie and drink orders—"but I gave up waiting for him to ask me. I gave so many hints!" Allegra sighed. "But Javier's fun. Hey, why don't I ask him to bring a friend, and we can all go together!"

Isa shook her head. "No, it's okay. You have a good time. I'll stay home and practice violin or help Jessie and Orlando with their science fair project."

"That just sounds sad," Allegra said. "Come with us. Homecoming won't be fun without you."

The customers in front of them finished their order and stepped to the side, and Allegra and Isa went to the counter. Isa peered at the cookie selections for the day. Her mom had recently perfected a new recipe: a delicious pecan molasses chocolate chunk cookie.

"Hey. I heard some homecoming talk," Jason said,

leaning his elbows against the counter. "Are you two going?"

"You know, we were just talking about that," Allegra said, smiling up at him. "I'm going with Javier. What about you?"

"I'm a little late on the planning," Jason said. "It's been so busy here, plus I've been trying to stay on top of schoolwork. But I was hoping to go. Isa, are you going?"

Allegra smiled gleefully as she looked at Isa. "I've been trying to convince her to go, but she's being difficult."

Jason stood up and started their drinks, not even having to ask what they wanted because they always ordered the same thing: hot chocolate, extra whip, with a dash of cinnamon and nutmeg on top. "Isa, we can go together, if you want," he said over his shoulder.

Isa blinked. "What?"

Jason turned back to the counter, two mugs in his hands. "We should go together. I promise to wear clothes that don't have your mom's bakery logo on them. You might not recognize me."

Isa just stared at him until Allegra jabbed her in the ribs.

Say yes, Allegra mouthed.

Isa wanted to say yes, but she couldn't get her mouth to form the word. Jason was great! He was funny and nice! And yet, she couldn't say the word.

"Let me think about it?" Isa said instead.

"If you're worried about your mom," Jason said, "she said it was okay. I already asked her if I could ask you."

"That is so nice," Allegra said with a sigh. "He already obtained parental consent."

"It's just that things are a little strange right now," Isa explained, not wanting Jason to think she didn't like him. "Our neighbor passed away last Friday. I don't know how much I'm in the mood for a dance."

"Hey, no problem," Jason said, putting a couple of cookies on a dish and sliding it over. Then he wrote his phone number on a Post-it Note and put it next to the cookies. "Call me when you decide."

"Thanks," Isa said, and they paid for their order.

Isa took the note and the cookies and Allegra took the hot chocolates, and when they got to their table, Allegra gave a little squeal of delight.

"Holy smokes, Jason Chu just asked you out," Allegra whisper-shouted at Isa. "Wait. I just need to sear this moment in my memory. What's his number? Can I plug it into my phone?"

Isa shoved the Post-it with Jason's number on it into her pencil case. "No. I don't want you texting him weird things about me."

Allegra put a hand on her chest. "*Moi?* Your best friend? Texting your boyfriend weird things about you?"

"Shhh!" Isa briefly dropped her head to the table. "He's definitely not my boyfriend. Geez, Allegra, get a grip."

Allegra looked back at Jason. "Too bad I already said yes to Javier . . ."

Isa shook her head. "I'm not even sure I want to go to homecoming."

Allegra sat down and stared at Isa. "You're not still holding out for Benny, are you? Because it sounds like—"

"I know," Isa interrupted. "I'm not waiting for him to ask anymore. Can we please stop talking about this? I need to get caught up on my homework so I can go home and practice violin."

Allegra did an eyebrow wiggle and rested her chin on her fingertips. "Stop being boring. Let's talk about Jason instead."

"No," Isa said, but she couldn't help smiling. She opened her books, grabbed a highlighter from her pencil case, and pointed it at Allegra. "Get to work."

Twenty-Four

It was an endless day at school, and Jessie felt as if she were wading through sand as she made her way to her classes. Once the high school bell rang, Jessie headed to the elementary school to pick up Oliver, Hyacinth, and Laney. Her siblings appeared to mirror her own mood: tired and listless. Even Laney had nothing to say when Jessie asked about her day. When they got to the brownstone, Laney snuggled under a blanket on the couch with Tuxedo and Paganini, while Oliver headed outside to the backyard to feed the chickens and do homework in his treehouse. Jessie assumed "homework" really meant that he would meet up with Angie and Jimmy L and eat candy. Hyacinth pulled out her yarn and needles and started knitting, which Jessie knew was her way of relaxing.

Jessie sat at the dining room table and pulled out her textbooks. She was going to tackle her English Lit homework first since that was the most boring. She wasn't a huge fan of the book they were reading, a novel set in the 1920s about people who seemed to be in love with each other when they shouldn't be. The story confused her, and she assumed she was reading it all wrong. She much preferred to read *National Geographic*, where all the stories were backed up by science. There was nothing bewildering about those stories.

An hour later, Jessie was ready to pound her head against the table. The book really was awful. She laid her cheek against the cool wood of the table, and that was how Mama found her when she came home at four o'clock.

"Hey," Mama said, resting a hand on Jessie's head. "Everything okay?"

"Just wonderful," said Jessie.

"You know what I think you need?" Mama asked.

"Some fresh air. I just saw Orlando and Mr. Beiderman head to track practice. Why don't you go to the park and yell encouraging words to them as they run?"

"That's a terrible idea," Jessie said, but she got up from the table anyway and headed for the front door.

"That's my girl," Mama said, helping Jessie put on her jacket and slipping a few homemade apple-cider caramels into her pocket. Mama then made her way to the couch, where Laney had fallen asleep with Tuxedo in her lap and Paganini nibbling at the hem of her T-shirt. "Invite Orlando and Mr. Beiderman for dinner," Mama said to Jessie. "I'll defrost a lasagna."

"Okay," Jessie said. She stepped out onto the sidewalk and took a deep breath. The smell of autumn met her nose: crunchy leaves and crisp apples and roasting vegetables. She headed toward the park, her hands buried deep in her pockets and her head tucked into her jacket.

As she walked by Harlem Coffee, Jessie looked through the windows and saw people sitting at the tables. They were typing away on their computers or drinking coffee and laughing with friends. She continued down the street, past a woman pushing a cart that had two bags of groceries and a group of people in medical scrubs heading into a bodega for a late-afternoon snack.

It was strange, Jessie thought as she continued to the park. The past few weeks had felt so completely disruptive, and yet time still passed and people went on with their lives. They hung out with their friends and walked their dogs and bought groceries. But for Jessie, life seemed utterly transformed. It made her think about Mr. Beiderman and how affected he had been by the death of his wife and daughter, Luciana. Mr. Beiderman, although trapped by grief for so many years, had found the strength to move on.

Jessie breathed in the autumn air, and for the first time in days, she felt a little light flicker on inside her. And when she reached the park and caught a glimpse of Mr. Beiderman, surrounded by Orlando and five other runners, the light became a little stronger. She stood by the coach, who was timing everyone's laps with a stopwatch and writing results on his clipboard. Occasionally, when he saw someone moving particularly slowly, he would yell, "Pick it up! I *will* run next to you and blow this dang whistle in your ear the whole time!"

Standing by the coach was a small group of people who cheered on runners as they passed by. As far as Jessie could tell, these people weren't related to any of the runners at all. They appeared to be hanging out for the sole purpose of encouraging the high school cross-country team.

Not too long after, she watched Mr. Beiderman as he completed another lap and passed by them again. And Jessie was surprised to find that he ran a lot better than when she had first seen him jog. Six months ago his shoulders hunched forward, his chin jutted out, and his feet shuffled. He did not inspire confidence that he could complete a marathon. But now his stride was nice and long and his head was in line with his body and his feet no longer dragged along the ground.

"Looking good, Mr. B!" Jessie yelled as he passed. Mr. B gave her a thumbs-up and Orlando did his cool chin-lift thing. She was amazed. Orlando was a miracle worker if he could turn reclusive, couch potato Mr. Beiderman into a marathon runner!

They went around a few more times, Jessie cheering them on each time. Was it possible that Mr. Beiderman would actually make it through the entire marathon? Not even once in the past six months had Jessie believed that he could finish the course. She felt a flush of pride at his progress over the past three years. When she had first met him, he hadn't left his apartment in six years. Now he was training for the biggest marathon in the world.

The runners were starting to cool off, and Jessie watched Mr. Beiderman and Orlando come her way. They were drinking from water bottles and looked to be in serious conversation. When they saw her, their faces lit up.

"Hey," Orlando said. "Thanks for coming out."

"Mama made me take a walk because I was in a terrible mood," Jessie said. "You looked good out there, Mr. B."

"I hate interval training," Mr. Beiderman replied.

"'Hate' is a strong word," Jessie chastised, imitating her mom's voice.

Mr. Beiderman scowled. "I have strong negative feelings about interval training."

"You did just fine," Jessie replied. "How did you get to be such an amazing runner?"

"Right?" Orlando said, taking another slug from his water bottle. "He's getting so good."

"On Sunday, get ready to have two million people cheering you on," Jessie said. "Laney is making you a shirt with your name on it so people will know to yell your name out."

Mr. Beiderman groaned. "I was hoping she had forgotten about that shirt."

"You're going to love it," Orlando said. "It will give you a boost when you're running. And it will help the cross-country team find you when we join you on the course."

"I want to wear this," Mr. Beiderman said, gesturing to his all-black workout clothes.

"No, no," Jessie said, wagging a finger at him. "Laney's heart would be broken."

"C'mon," Orlando said. "It'll be fun. People wear all sorts of funny things when they run the marathon. Chicken costumes. Superhero outfits complete with fake muscles. Business suits. A T-shirt with your name on it will look tame in comparison."

"Laney has been excited about making your marathon shirt for weeks," Jessie reminded him.

"Fine," Mr. B grumbled. "I'll wear it."

Jessie smiled. "Good. Also, this might be a good time for me to warn you that she's putting a *lot* of glitter on it."

Mr. Beiderman sighed, and Jessie and Orlando laughed. It was the first time she had laughed or heard Orlando laugh in a week, and it felt good to let herself be happy, if only for a few moments.

WEDNESDAY, OCTOBER 30

Four Days Until the New York City Marathon

Twenty-Five

In all the heartache of the past week, the Vanderbeekers had almost forgotten about the Halloween 5K Fun Run they'd organized for October 31. Oliver had first gotten the idea that summer when they'd learned that Mr. Beiderman was hard at work training for the marathon. After a lengthy family meeting during which they discussed the probability of Mr. Beiderman's finishing the 26.2-mile course (Jessie calculated the chance for success at 2.4 percent), they decided it might be nice to have a practice 5K run beforehand. The probability of him completing a 5K, which was just over three miles, was much higher.

When the Vanderbeekers had looked at the calendar to schedule the 5K, they were happily surprised to find that the New York City marathon was just a few days after Halloween, which made October 31 the perfect day to do the fun run. People could run in costume, which meant that some might also dress up their pets, an idea that greatly appealed to all of them.

Papa had chatted with some of the running groups in Harlem (they all loved the idea) and then coordinated with the Parks Department and the City College of New York (they also loved the idea), and the Halloween 5K was born.

It was only when Oliver, Laney, and Hyacinth went to school that morning that they were reminded of the event. Everyone was talking about their costumes. Thankfully, Hyacinth had prepared costumes a month ago; the Vanderbeekers, Mr. Beiderman, and Orlando were dressing up as a BLT sandwich, only in place of bacon they were substituting avocado because Hyacinth and Laney refused to eat bacon since it came from pigs.

Hyacinth had procured large sheets of brown, green, and red felt, as well as foam core, and had transformed them into slices of bread, a slice of avocado, and a round tomato. Laney was going to wear a frilly green dress and call herself lettuce, Mama and Papa would be the bread slices, and Hyacinth and Oliver flipped a coin to see who would be the remaining fixings. (No one wanted to be the tomato.)

Oliver had lost the coin toss, and Hyacinth tried to make the tomato as visually pleasing as possible for him. When it was done, Oliver reluctantly put his costume on and proclaimed that he looked like target practice. Mama said he looked adorable, which made him feel even worse.

But a deal was a deal. Oliver had hoped that Hyacinth would forget about the fun run, but it appeared now to be the one thing that excited her after the sadness of the previous weeks. Jessie, Orlando, and Mr. Beiderman were dressing up as condiments: ketchup, mustard, and sriracha. Isa and Miss Josie flatly refused to either dress up or run; they volunteered to greet finishers with cups of water and Halloween candy instead.

✧ ✧ ✧

At school, Hyacinth took out her knitting at recess and sat in her usual spot on top of the storage bins, which was a quiet, sunny place to spend twenty minutes before going back to her chaotic classroom. A couple of minutes later, Maria joined her with her own bag of knitting.

"Look what I have," Maria said, opening the bag so Hyacinth could see inside.

"Wow," Hyacinth said, looking at five skeins of yarn and a few different sizes of knitting needles.

"And," Maria continued, "I finished the square I was working on, and you can have your needles back because my grandma gave me some of hers and all this yarn. She says she wants to meet you because she's never been able to get me into knitting and she's surprised you were able to convince me it's fun."

Hyacinth smiled.

"Seriously, though," Maria said. "She wants to meet you. She's bringing me to the fun run tomorrow. Do you have a costume?"

Hyacinth nodded and told Maria about their sandwich costume.

Maria sighed. "My parents were supposed to get me a costume, but they ended up having to work. My grandma said she'd take me to Goodwill this afternoon, but I doubt they'll have any costumes this close to Halloween."

"Maybe you can be a part of our sandwich," Hyacinth said. "You can be, um, hmm . . ."

"It's okay," Maria said, pulling out the light-green square she was working on. "I'll think of something."

"I know!" Hyacinth said, her eyes lingering on the green yarn. "You can be alfalfa sprouts! We can make a bunch of finger knitting and drape it all over you!"

Maria shook her head. "Wouldn't that take a long time? We already have this big quilt to finish."

"Oh, finger knitting is so quick and easy," Hyacinth said. "We could make your costume fast. I'll show you."

Maria had a ball of white yarn, so Hyacinth showed her how to wrap the yarn around her fingers to create a long chain coming down. By the time recess ended, they had ten six-inch strands. Now they just needed to wrap the top of each strand with light-green yarn, and it would look exactly like an alfalfa sprout. Then they could sew them all to a shirt.

"Thanks for letting me be a vegetable in your sandwich," Maria said with a happy smile.

"The more veggies in our sandwich," Hyacinth said, "the better."

When the bell rang, the two new friends headed back to their classrooms. Halfway across the blacktop, Maria looped her arm through Hyacinth's, and for the first time in weeks, Hyacinth felt hope bloom in her chest.

Thursday, October 31

Three Days Until the New York City Marathon

Twenty-Six

The next day, Laney waited anxiously for Isa to pick her up after school so she could get into her costume. Maria, Hyacinth's friend, was coming home with them, and her grandma would meet her at the finish line.

The route would begin on 141st Street at St. Nicholas Avenue, proceed up a steep hill to Convent Avenue, then go through City College's campus. The course then cut across St. Nicholas Park and ended with a set of stone stairs that led to the finish line. Finishers would be greeted with water, lots of candy, and a dance party.

Laney could not wait to get dressed up!

As the lettuce, Laney knew she had the best cos-

5K Route

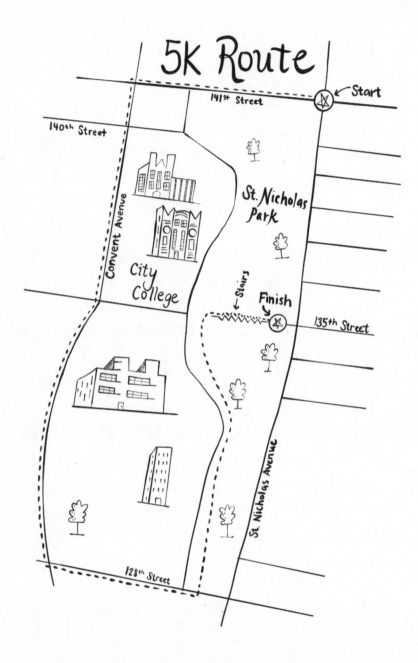

Start

141st Street

140th Street

Convent Avenue

St. Nicholas Park

City College

Stairs

Finish

135th Street

St. Nicholas Avenue

128th Street

tume of all. Her dress was frilly, to make it look as if she were wearing green leaf lettuce, and the light fabric fluttered when she ran. She wanted to wear a pair of white boots with her outfit, but Mama insisted that she wear something she could run in, so she put on a pair of green sneakers that had belonged to Hyacinth and, before that, Oliver.

"I'm ready!" Laney said as she skipped down the stairs in her outfit. Tuxedo followed, batting at the flowing panels of her dress.

"I don't know how I'm going to run in this," Oliver said, gesturing to his large felt tomato costume.

"It'll be easier than running in *this*," Jessie said, wearing a green hat, which was supposed to be the top of the sriracha bottle, and a narrow red dress that went down to her ankles. She shuffled along, restricted from her regular stride.

A door opening and closing on next floor gave way to the sound of Mr. Beiderman clomping down the stairs in his mustard costume.

"Whose idea was this, anyway?" he asked. "I don't even like mustard."

"You know we organized this fun run especially for

you," Hyacinth told him, pinning a last alfalfa sprout to Maria's shirt. "A warm-up before the big day."

"I *love* my costume," Maria piped up, showing off her shirt, which had yarn alfalfa sprouts yarn sewn all over it.

"How do I look?" Orlando said as he emerged from the bathroom dressed as a ketchup bottle, his arms splayed wide.

Hyacinth flashed him a thumbs-up; then everyone was ordered to gather for a group photo in front of the brownstone. Mama and Papa (the bread pieces) stood on either side of Oliver, Hyacinth, Laney, and Maria in their respective tomato, avocado, lettuce, and alfalfa-sprout costumes. Next to them were the condiments: Jessie, Orlando, and Mr. Beiderman as sriracha, ketchup, and mustard.

After Isa had taken dozens of photos on everyone's phone per Mama's request, and Miss Josie had taken a whole roll of photos on her ancient point-and-shoot camera, the costumed runners got ready to leave while Isa and Miss Josie went back inside to load up the Radio Flyer wagon with the Halloween cookies Mama had made that morning.

"Mr. Jeet would have loved this," Miss Josie said, blinking rapidly as tears formed in her eyes.

Isa wrapped her arms around her neighbor. "Would you rather stay at home? I can manage the cookies and water on my own."

"Nonsense," said Miss Josie, putting the large bakery boxes of cookies on top of the cooler. "I need to get out and keep moving. It would be too easy for me to stay at home, feeling sad."

Miss Josie held out her arm and Isa linked it with hers, and together they made their way down 141st Street toward the park.

Twenty-Seven

The Vanderbeekers and their friends gathered at the starting line on 141st and St. Nicholas. Orlando's cross-country team was there, having decided that they would do the fun run instead of having practice. They'd wrapped toilet paper around themselves to look like mummies but must have done a hasty job because toilet paper was falling off and ripping off in various sections, revealing their running clothes underneath.

Oliver kept an eye out for his friends, and finally he spotted Angie and Jimmy L in their basketball jerseys.

"You guys didn't dress up?" Oliver asked, now feeling supremely self-conscious about being a tomato.

"We're dressed up as basketball players," Angie said with a shrug.

"Isn't that cheating?" Oliver asked, looking at her jersey. "I mean, that's what you normally wear."

"Yeah, but it's also a costume. There are plenty of kids wearing leotards and ballerina skirts," Angie pointed out.

"But they don't wear that to school or as their normal clothes. That's basically your life uniform."

Angie shrugged again, then gestured toward the starting line. "C'mon, let's get to the front so we don't get stuck behind the little kids."

Oliver, Angie, and Jimmy L made their way to the front of the line, where Orlando, Mr. Beiderman, and the high school cross-country team were stretching.

"Ah, competition," Orlando said to his team as he saw the trio heading his way. "Watch out, people. These kids are fast."

"I'm sure we can beat them," a guy with round glasses said with a grin.

"I'm sure you could," Angie said easily, bringing her knee up to stretch her hamstring.

"What?" Oliver said, offended at Angie's lack of faith in their running. "I think—"

"I mean," Angie continued, "how could a few lowly sixth graders beat a top-ranked high school cross-country team?"

"No offense," commented a cross-country guy with dark-brown hair, "but you could never beat us. We're too good."

Angie nodded in agreement. "That's probably true, but it would be good to race your team anyway. You know, to get experience. Maybe we can bet you something . . . like if we win, you have to go trick-or-treating with us and then give us all of your Halloween candy."

The cross-country team laughed.

"Aw, these kids are so cute," the guy in the glasses said. "What will you do if we win?"

"We would give you all of our Halloween candy, of course. Orlando can bring it to you tomorrow."

The guy with dark-brown hair shrugged. "I don't see any harm in a little competition," he said. "As long as you don't cry when you lose."

Orlando, who remained silent during this whole exchange, caught the gleam in Angie's eyes. He grinned and leaned toward Jessie. "This should be interesting."

Angie and the guy with glasses shook hands, and Angie took her place between Oliver and Jimmy L.

"Why would you give away all of our Halloween candy?" Oliver angry-whispered from the side of his mouth.

"Chill out, Oliver," Angie said. "Think about it: we've been training with the high school basketball team for the last couple of weeks. We're way stronger now."

"But these guys are *runners*," Oliver said. "They know what they're doing!"

Angie shrugged. "So do we."

Papa's voice over a bullhorn got everyone's attention. "Welcome to the first annual Halloween Five-K Fun Run in Harlem! We're so excited to see you all here. Please follow the course carefully; there will be people stationed throughout to make sure you're going in the right direction. We'll have a dance party at the finish line, so be ready to show off your best moves. Is everyone ready?"

The runners—people dressed up as superheroes

and ballerinas and athletes and goblins and witches and sandwiches—cheered. Their pets, wearing dinosaur, lion, and shark costumes, howled in displeasure.

"On your marks, get set, *GO!*"

Oliver, Jimmy L, and Angie started off strong, even though Oliver had to navigate around his huge costume.

"Don't slow us down, Oliver!" Angie yelled as she worked her way up the steep hill toward City College.

"You try running while wearing a huge tomato!" Oliver huffed.

"No excuses!" Angie called.

Oliver glanced back to see that the high school cross-country runners were not far behind but were a little distracted by their rapidly unraveling mummy costumes. The road to City College was steep, and from his vantage point halfway up, Oliver could get a good look at the long waves of people laughing and huffing and struggling to the top of the hill. He spotted Herman Huxley with Hyacinth and Maria way at the bottom, holding on to leashes attached to Franz and Billie Holiday. They were trying to coax Franz up the hill, but the portly basset hound was not a fan of his shark costume or of the steep walk. Many people had made the fun run into a fun walk, and they rambled up the hill in their brightly colored costumes, chatting and laughing and enjoying the gorgeous fall weather.

Oliver turned back as he passed Alexander Hamilton's house on his left. The yellow house with white trim sat surrounded by grass with a big National Memorial sign attached to the surrounding fence. Oliver was starting to get winded, and Angie, sensing that he was slowing down, yelled at him again. Oliver sucked in a breath of air and forced his legs to keep moving. His thigh hit the bottom of the tomato with each stride, which caused the costume to bounce uncomfortably on his neck and bang into his chin.

Once they got to the entrance of City College, the course flattened out and Oliver felt better. Running was easier now, and he caught up with Angie and Jimmy L.

"We're going to have to bring up the speed in a second," Angie said, looking over her shoulder.

"Why—" Jimmy L began, then looked back and said, "Oh no."

Oliver glanced back. The entire pack of cross-country runners, led by the guy in the dark-rimmed glasses, was a few paces away. Their mummy costumes hung in shreds around them, and they looked like evil, grinning zombies.

"Pick it up!" Angie yelled.

Oliver could hear the runners behind him, the steady pounding of their sneakers hitting the pavement. Even though his lungs were burning, he ran faster as they entered St. Nicholas Park.

"Think of the candy!" Angie called out, her ponytail bobbing in front of him.

"Think about how we're going to *lose* all of our candy!" Jimmy L said as he ran next to Oliver.

Oliver was so winded that he couldn't talk, so he started counting in his head. *I just need to run until I get to one hundred,* he told himself.

"We're almost there!" Angie said as she turned right to go down a long set of stone stairs to the finish line. A red ribbon was stretched across the end of the route, and it looked as if she would be the first to reach it. Oliver, however, could practically feel the breath of a high school mummy on his neck.

As he made his way down the stairs, Oliver's legs turned to jelly. He lagged behind Angie and Jimmy L, and then he was head-to-head with one of the cross-country runners. He was passed once, then again. Oliver did *not* want to be the reason for losing a whole stash of candy, so he made his legs move faster. He passed the cross-country runners, and then they gained the lead over him again. Angie and Jimmy L were close to the finish line, and Oliver knew he had to put on a burst of speed or they would lose.

The two high school runners took up the width of the stone stairs in front of him, making it impossible for him to pass. To the side was a grassy hill that descended to the bottom of the park, so Oliver decided to go around them.

Because the grass was slippery from the rain earlier that day, and also because tree roots and acorns and pinecones were abundant, this detour turned out to be a big mistake. Oliver slipped on a pinecone and down he went, his feet sliding out from under him. And then, because his costume was so beautifully round as a result of Hyacinth's costume-making skills, he rolled down the hill at a record rate.

Oliver thought he would never stop, but then a massive pile of leaves that the Parks Department had left by the curb swallowed him up. A cheer rose from the crowd when he came to rest.

"Oh my gosh! Oliver, are you okay?" came muffled voices.

Oliver sat up to find Isa, Miss Josie, Angie, and Jimmy L surrounding him, eyeing him in concern.

"I think so," Oliver said, dazed.

"That was *epic*," Jimmy L said. "Just incredible."

Isa reached over and plucked some leaves from his hair. "That costume made you go down the hill so fast I was afraid you would roll right into the street!"

"We won!" Angie yelled, jumping up and down. "We beat a regionally ranked cross-country team!"

Oliver looked around. The high school team was scowling in his direction.

"We did it!" Oliver said, hopping up and high-fiving his friends. "Candy for eternity!"

He cheered and ripped off his tomato costume. He was never, ever going to be a tomato again.

Friday, November 1

Two Days Until the New York City Marathon

Twenty-Eight

On Friday morning, everyone woke up a little groggy. The night before, Oliver, Angie, and Jimmy L had gone trick-or-treating with Orlando, Jessie, and the cross-country team for three hours, and they'd returned to the brownstone with enough candy to last for years. They lugged the bags up to the treehouse, stashing it away before Mama could confiscate it.

"We're rich!" Angie had said as she dug into the pile of candy in the hidden storage bin, then let it fall through her hands as if she were a pirate reveling in treasure.

Now that the festivities were over, Oliver dragged himself out of bed, feeling absolutely wretched from all the candy he had eaten the day before.

He brushed his teeth and went downstairs to the kitchen, where Mama was dishing out yogurt and fruit. Laney was just finishing her breakfast when he arrived.

"I'm going upstairs to Miss Josie's," Laney announced as she hopped off her stool.

"You are?" said Mama, Papa, and Oliver.

"Yup," Laney responded. "Why? Is something wrong?"

And then Oliver noticed something about Laney: she wasn't wearing her usual chewed-up turtleneck. It had been months since he had seen her wear something other than the turtleneck.

Mama put her arm around Laney. "Nothing is wrong, sweetie," she said. "It's just that you haven't gone up to the second floor since Mr. Jeet passed away."

"Miss Josie asked me to," Laney said. "We decided that we're going to take a walk together once a day to visit the garden and add new memories if we think of them." Laney held up a fistful of fabric strips.

"I love that idea," Papa said, leaning down to kiss her cheek.

"Miss Josie said that she felt so sad about Mr. Jeet that she didn't want to get out of bed in the morning, which is exactly how I felt. And then she told me she wanted to keep all her memories about Mr. Jeet, and *then* she asked me how the garden was looking. And I said it was looking nice, and maybe she would want to come and see it with me. And Miss Josie said yes, and then she said maybe we should go there every day to see how the memory fence looks. And that's why I'm going upstairs. Because we both miss Mr. Jeet, but when we're together, we feel better."

And with that, Laney gathered up Paganini and marched to the first floor. They heard the door open and close, and then faint footsteps as Laney continued to the second floor.

Oliver sat and stared at the bowl of yogurt Mama set next to him. As he prepared to take his first bite, Hyacinth, Isa, and Jessie came down the stairs.

"What are you going to wear for homecoming to-morrow?" Jessie asked Isa. "Please tell me you're not wearing that horrid orange dress. No offense, but it makes you look like a pumpkin. Not that Benjamin cares what you wear. He thinks you look good in everything."

Isa helped herself to yogurt and fruit, then sat in her usual seat. "Actually, I'm not going to homecoming with Benny."

Mama dropped the cup she was washing in the sink. "What did you say?"

Papa looked as if Christmas had come early. "You're not going to the dance? Well, that's wonderful! If you're going to hang around here tomorrow, let's plan a movie night. You choose the movie, I'll make the popcorn. Jessie, you're not going either, right? We can have some father-daughter ti—"

"Papa," Isa interrupted. "I'm going with Jason."

Papa's mouth dropped open. "Jason? As in Jason-who-works-at-the-Treehouse-Bakery-Jason?"

"Why would you do that?" Jessie asked, horrified. "Jason is so . . . so . . ."

"I like Jason," Oliver interjected. "He has cool shoes."

"I like Jason too," Mama said. "He's a nice kid. I mean, I *did* hire him. He asked me if he could take you."

"He did?" Papa asked, his eyes swiveling to stare at Mama. "Wait, what am I missing? What happened to Benjamin?"

"Benny is going with someone else," Isa said, carrying her bowl to the sink and nudging her mom out of the way so she could wash it. "I don't want to talk about it." She wiped her hands on the nearest kitchen towel, then packed her bag.

Oliver kept his mouth shut. After all, he hadn't lived around his sisters for eleven years without learning a thing or two. He watched Isa get her backpack ready and said goodbye to her when she left for school. What he really wanted to say was "What's the big deal? Jason's cool!" But some inner voice told him that it would be the exact wrong thing to say.

✦ ✦ ✦

Isa was not surprised when she had another absolutely terrible day. School had been awful ever since she had spotted Benny hanging out with that girl a week earlier. She found herself nervous to look too intently around the halls, afraid that she would see him with the mystery girl, or worse, that he would catch her alone, which would mean she would have to talk to him. What would she say?

Her fears were fully realized when the last bell rang and she headed to her locker to get the books she needed for the weekend. Allegra wasn't waiting for her; she hadn't been feeling well and had left school early. Isa was putting her last book into her backpack when she heard that familiar "Hey."

She didn't dare turn around.

Benny leaned against the locker next to her. "I feel like we haven't spent time together in forever."

"Yeah," Isa said.

"You've been really busy," Benny said as he looked at her.

Isa let her hair fall in front of her so he couldn't see her face. "You've been busy too."

"How are you feeling, with Mr. Jeet and everything . . . ?" He trailed off.

"We're doing okay," Isa said, zipping up her backpack.

"Cool," Benny said.

Then a girl's voice echoed down the school hallway. "Benny, hurry! We're going to be late!"

"Gotta go," Benny said. "I'll see you soon, right?"

Isa glanced in the direction of the voice. That same girl was standing there with her hands on her hips, glaring at them. Isa looked back at Benny. She used to feel so comfortable with him, and now she had nothing to say except "Bye, Benny."

He jogged down the hall to join up with his friend, maybe girlfriend. Isa turned on her heel and headed the opposite direction. It was time to move on.

Stepping out of school, Isa paused right outside the door to feel the sun touch her face. Then she headed toward the cat café.

SATURDAY, NOVEMBER 2

One Day Until the New York City Marathon

Twenty-Nine

On the evening before the New York City Marathon, the whole cross-country team came to the Vanderbeekers for a pre-race dinner with Mr. Beiderman. Since the homecoming dance was also that night, Mama had planned an early meal so those who were going to the dance would have enough time to get ready. She cooked most of the day, making food she had carefully researched and found to be good for runners. All sorts of homemade pasta with anchovy and garlic, pesto, and red sauce, plus huge bowls of roasted vegetables, filled their dining room table. When the doorbell rang at four thirty, Papa opened the door to find Orlando and the cross-country team. Franz weaved between their ankles and rubbed his head against their sneakers.

Papa's eyes widened. "We're supposed to feed *all* of you?"

The cross-country team laughed good-naturedly and trickled inside. They greeted the Vanderbeeker kids, gave Oliver a special fist bump, met all the animals, and said hi to Mr. Beiderman and Miss Josie. After the formalities had been exchanged, the team converged around the table, grabbing plates and utensils and serving themselves massive amounts of food.

"Wow," Oliver said, watching them heap pasta on their plates. He stared longingly at the anchovy and garlic pasta, which happened to be his favorite. "Do you think there will be anything left when they're done?"

"I don't think so," Laney said, standing on a chair so she could update her siblings on the state of the dining room table. "They're taking so much!"

The cross-country team finally moved away from the food and filled the living room, sprawling out on couches or on the rug. They quickly learned to shoo away Tuxedo (who was notorious for stealing pasta), and they made lots of noise talking and laughing and teasing.

The Vanderbeekers, meanwhile, looked forlornly at the ravaged table, which held little but empty dishes.

"Pizza it is," Jessie said, taking out her phone to dial their local pizzeria. "That stinks. I've been looking forward to pasta all day."

"Hold on one second," Mama said as she disappeared into the closet that held the washer and dryer. She emerged with a platter of pasta.

"This one is anchovy and garlic," she said with a wink. "There's another with red sauce in there."

The Vanderbeekers happily filled their plates and sat in the living room with Mr. Beiderman and the cross-country team.

Laney took a seat next to Mr. Beiderman and twirled strands of spaghetti around her fork. "At school, Pedro said his uncle ran a marathon and there was lots of poop on the course. Like, people just poop while they're running!"

Mr. Beiderman looked up, startled, as if he were surprised to find himself sitting in this very loud living room surrounded by dozens of people. "Oh," he said.

One of the guys on the cross-country team sitting next to Laney choked on his mouthful of spaghetti.

Mr. Beiderman coughed. "I'm not worried about that."

"You'll be great!" Laney said. "We'll cheer you at Fifty-Ninth Street and then Ninety-Sixth Street and then a Hundred and Thirty-Eighth Street, and we'll be at the finish line to help you get home! Papa put an app on his phone that will track you. And look . . . I have a special surprise for you!" From behind the couch, she whipped a box bedazzled to the extreme with plastic gemstones, glitter, and puffy stickers.

Mr. Beiderman looked at it warily. "I'm afraid I'll be covered in glitter if I touch it."

"I'll open it!" Laney said, lifting the lid with a flourish and showering Mr. B in sparkles as she did so.

Inside the box was the flashiest purple running shirt imaginable. It made the box look boring by comparison. Sequins on the front spelled out "Cheer for Me! I'm Mr. B!" Feathers were sewn along the neckline, and dozens of large, mirror-like discs were sewn indiscriminately all around.

"The discs will reflect the light and be super sparkly when you run!" Laney said, hopping around in excitement. "Do you love it?" she asked Mr. Beiderman.

Mr. Beiderman glanced around; the Vanderbeekers and the cross-country team looked back at him expectantly.

"I, uh, love it," Mr. Beiderman said.

"Put it on!" Laney said.

"I think I'll save it for tomorrow," Mr. Beiderman said, but then everyone started chanting, "Put it on! Put it on!"

Mr. Beiderman sighed loudly; then he layered Laney's shirt over his black shirt and held out his arms. "How do I look?"

Mama, Papa, and Miss Josie suddenly found themselves very busy gathering dirty cups, and the cross-country team found their own sneakers fascinating. Oliver gave Mr. Beiderman a thumbs-down, but no one could see him because he was standing in the back by the food table.

"Perfect!" Laney said, clapping her hands.

After Mr. Beiderman and Miss Josie retreated to their apartments, the cross-country team headed to the kitchen to help Papa load the dirty dishes. Mama sent them away, saying that they should spiff themselves up for the dance and that her family would take care of cleanup.

"Does that mean us?" Oliver said, eyeing the mounds of dishes on the kitchen counters.

"Many hands make light work, or whatever," Jessie said, then looked at Isa. "Hey, you go get ready for the dance. I'm volunteering Orlando to do your share of the work."

Isa picked up the sponge and put dishwashing soap on it. "Actually, I'm not going."

"What?" asked Jessie, Hyacinth, Laney, Mama, and Papa.

"I mean, it's totally okay if plans have changed," added Mama quickly.

"It's just that we thought you *were* going," Papa added.

"With Jason," Jessie finished.

Isa shrugged. "I thought about it, but then I realized I didn't really want to. He's super nice and all, he's just not . . ."

Since Isa was facing the sink, Laney couldn't see her face, but she could hear a sadness in her sister's voice.

"I'm totally fine," Isa continued, as if hearing

Laney's thoughts. "Come on, let's get this done, and then we can make popcorn with Papa."

Papa grinned. "My heart just grew ten sizes." He grabbed a second sponge and took up the spot next to Isa at the double sink, filling a basin with warm water and adding dish detergent to it so it bubbled nicely.

Mama put on her 'Happy Beats' playlist and cranked up the volume, and the Vanderbeekers took their places in the assembly line. Papa dunked the dishes in the soapy water and handed them to Isa for scrubbing and rinsing. Jessie and Orlando then rubbed them dry with dish towels and passed them to Hyacinth and Laney, who were in charge of putting them away. Papa insisted that Mama take a break from dish duty, but Mama didn't want to sit around watching everyone clean without her, so she stood at the oven, scouring the stovetop until it gleamed.

Laney, Hyacinth, Mama, and Papa sang and danced along with the music while they worked. Even Isa started singing when a song she really liked came on. When Papa got to the last of the dishes, he drained the dirty water and started rinsing the basin with fresh water and soap. While he was rinsing it, however, the basin slipped from his hands, spilling soapy water all over Isa on its way to the floor.

Isa shrieked as the water drenched her clothes and splashed her face.

"Papa!" Isa squealed.

"I'm so sorry!" Papa said, his eyes wide. "It was an accident!"

Oliver coughed into his hand while saying, "Lies!" and that was all it took to trigger the Great Water War.

What ensued was a water fight of a magnitude never before seen on 141st Street. Oliver, who was always prepared in times of water battle, ran to the bathroom and emerged with a whole bucket of water balloons that he had stashed behind the washing machine for just such an occasion.

"Take it outside!" Mama screeched as she was nailed with a water balloon.

The Vanderbeekers and Orlando raced outside, Laney slipping a little on the wet kitchen floor and almost squashing Tuxedo. Jessie pulled out the hose and sprayed her family with abandon. Oliver made his way up to the treehouse and hammered people with water balloons. Franz leaped through the backyard, shaking water off himself and howling with glee. The chickens, surprised to find their quiet backyard invaded by water warriors, squawked and fled to safety in their coop.

Fifteen minutes later, Oliver finally ran out of water balloons and everyone was out of breath from running and laughing. Mama dashed inside to get towels. After they had dried themselves off, they went back inside the brownstone to clean up the kitchen and take showers.

Laney, who had managed to get soaked as well as completely covered in mud, was being ushered upstairs for her nighttime bath when she caught sight of a familiar face peering into the apartment through the living room window.

A second later, the doorbell rang.

Thirty

Isa was wiping smears of mud from her face and neck when Papa opened the door.

"*This* is a surprise," Papa said.

Isa glanced up and saw Benny silhouetted in the doorway.

Dressed in a suit, a purple tie, and dress shoes, Benny held a corsage in his hand.

"Wow, you look so fancy," Laney said.

"What are you doing here?" Papa asked him, crossing his arms.

"Sir? I, uh . . ." He glanced past Papa's shoulder and looked at Isa. "I'm here to pick up Isa for the homecoming dance?"

Isa couldn't get a full sentence to form in her mouth. "What? I thought—but—You never asked. You have a girlfriend . . ." She trailed off.

"A girlfriend?" Benny said, his brow creased in confusion. "What girlfriend?"

There was a long period of quiet when everyone just stared at each other.

"Oh boy, this is going to be *good*," Oliver said. Laney settled down next to him on the stairs.

Jessie yanked Oliver by the shirt. "This is not entertainment," she announced. "Up we go."

"But—" Laney protested.

"Aww," Oliver said, but he followed Orlando, who'd slung Laney over his shoulder and headed up the stairs.

"Come on, Hyacinth," Jessie said.

Hyacinth whistled to Franz. "Let's go visit Miss Josie!" she said, scuttling up the stairs behind her siblings, Franz's claws clicking against the hardwood floor.

That left wet and disheveled Mama, Papa, and Isa staring at Benny.

"Uh, I think there's been a misunderstanding," Benny began, glancing at the three remaining Vanderbeekers.

"You think?" Papa said, his arms still crossed.

Isa regained her ability to talk. She looked at Benny. "You're right. I don't understand. You never asked me to homecoming. I thought you were going with someone else."

"I was never going with someone else! And I did ask you," Benny said, then he paused to consider. "Didn't I?"

"No," Isa said.

Benny tried again. "But we've gone to every dance together for the last year and a half. I assumed we would go to this one."

"You still have to ask," Mama advised.

"You've been with another girl these past couple of weeks," Isa said. "You two were talking about homecoming on the way to class, so I just assumed . . ."

". . . that I was dating some girl without even saying anything to you?" Benny said. "I would never do that!"

"Well," Mama said, heading toward the laundry

room and collecting the wet towels on the floor. "I think I'll just throw these wet towels in the wash."

"Okay," Papa said, not budging from his spot between Isa and Benny. Then he saw the look on Mama's face and followed her to the laundry room, closing the door with a click.

"Who is she?" Isa asked.

"Who?" Benny said.

"That girl you've been hanging out with!" Isa said, exasperated. "The one I thought you were dating. The tall one. Always flicking her hair over her shoulders."

"Oh, ick, you thought I was dating *Imogene?*" Benny said, his face horrified. "She's my *cousin!* You've met her before, haven't you? She comes into the city a few times a year. She just moved here permanently a couple of weeks ago, and my parents asked me to make sure she adjusted well and everything. But she can be sort of . . . prickly, so she's had a hard time making friends. I felt bad abandoning her at school."

Isa searched her memory for a person named Imogene, and now that she thought about it, the name did sound familiar. "But you two were talking about homecoming . . ."

Benny shuddered. "I can't believe you thought I was taking my *cousin* to homecoming! She had asked me to help her find a date. Maybe that's what you heard?"

Isa let out a relieved sigh. "I guess when you didn't ask me, and then I saw you hanging out with her nonstop and talking about the dance . . . I should have asked you about it."

"I'm sorry," Benny said, his eyes remorseful. He held out the corsage. "Forgive me?"

Isa smiled and took the corsage. "I forgive you."

Benny put his hands in his pockets and shifted from foot to foot. "So, are you ready to go to the dance, or do you want to change?"

Isa's hands flew up to her hair. "Oh my gosh, I am such a mess!"

"We'll help you get ready!" Hyacinth yelled from above.

Isa looked up. Her siblings and Orlando were at the top of the stairs, their heads peeking over the top of the railing.

"You can use my glitter!" called Laney. "We can

sprinkle it in your hair and you'll look like a fairy princess!"

"Just don't wear that orange dress," Jessie said. "That orange dress is just . . . no."

"I'm never going to a school dance," Oliver declared, and Franz woofed in agreement.

Mama and Papa came out of the laundry room, Isa ran upstairs to get washed up, and Oliver made Benjamin go outside to practice basketball drills with him in front of the brownstone until Isa was finished. Twenty minutes later—with the help of Jessie, Hyacinth, Laney, and Mama—Isa dashed down the stairs and poked her head out the front door.

"I'm ready!" Isa called.

Benny abandoned the ball mid-drill and let it roll under a parked car. Oliver grumbled as the basketball got stuck between the undercarriage of the car and the pavement. He had to knock it free using a broom handle. Mama and Papa took the requisite pre-dance photos, and off Isa and Benny went to the dance.

As they watched them go down the street, Papa

wrapped his arms around Mama and kissed the top of her head. "I love you," he said.

"I love you too," Mama said.

"Ick," Oliver said. Mama reached out, and Oliver put his basketball under his arm and let himself be hugged.

As Oliver looked up at his parents, he caught sight of one of the brownstone windows on the second floor. Miss Josie was sitting there with a haunted look on her face. When Oliver followed her line of sight, he realized she was looking at Orlando, who was sitting on the stoop with Jessie. When Oliver looked up at the window to see Miss Josie's face again, she was gone.

Thirty-One

After giving Isa and Benjamin a proper sendoff, Jessie and Orlando went down to the basement to work on their science project. Jessie wondered whether she should bring up the impending deadline for Orlando's decision as she watched him create a spreadsheet for testing their hypothesis. He appeared tired from the events of the last month, but when he caught her watching him, he flashed his signature grin.

"Watch and learn as I create the ultimate spreadsheet for true scientific inquiry." Orlando cracked his knuckles and turned back to the computer.

Jessie glanced over his shoulder and gave him some suggestions, and a few minutes later they had a good-looking chart.

"This is cause for celebration!" Jessie said, leading the way upstairs, where the smell of popcorn was wafting through the brownstone. Laney was standing on a step stool, drizzling chocolate into a bowl filled with freshly popped corn.

Hyacinth was sprinkling Parmesan on top of popcorn in another bowl, and Papa was at the stove with the ancient iron corn popper, cranking the handle that rotated the kernels inside.

"It's nice outside," Jessie said. "Should we do a REP Movie Night?"

Papa looked as if someone had just given him season tickets for his favorite basketball team.

"It's Hyacinth's turn to choose a movie," Laney announced, and everyone groaned. Hyacinth was so empathetic that all but one movie terrified her. She always selected *Babe,* the story of a pig living on a farm in England.

The Vanderbeekers grabbed Mama from the couch, where she was happily buried in a pile of throw blankets, reading a novel and drinking tea. They forced her upstairs, through Isa and Jessie's bedroom window, and up the fire escape. Tapping on Miss Josie's window as they passed by, they asked if she wanted to join them, but she shook her head and pointed to the television, where *Jeopardy!* was on. Miss Josie loved *Jeopardy!*

Pretty soon the Vanderbeekers were relaxing in the Adirondack chairs with bowls of popcorn in their laps. Before Jessie pressed play, Orlando stepped in front of the projection screen and cleared his throat.

"Can I just say something before the movie begins?" he asked.

Everyone nodded, and Jessie's stomach dropped. He was going to tell them he was going back to Georgia; she knew it. As she braced herself, Orlando's words registered in her head.

"I'm going to stay here with Miss Josie," he said.

Hyacinth, Laney, Oliver, and Jessie sprang from their seats, popcorn bowls upended, and rushed to him for hugs.

"I knew it, I knew it!" Laney said. "I knew you couldn't leave us!"

"This is the best news *ever!*" Hyacinth exclaimed.

"Now you can help me train for basketball tryouts!" Oliver said.

"Science fair reigning champions, here we come!" Jessie said. "Oh my gosh, Miss Josie must be so excited."

Orlando grinned. "I told her yesterday, but I think she filled out the guardianship paperwork last week in hopes I would say yes."

Once the Vanderbeeker kids were done jumping all over Orlando, Mama and Papa came to give him hugs.

"We're so glad, Orlando," Mama said.

"We love you, Orlando," Papa said. "Don't ever forget that."

If Jessie had been watching her parents' faces more closely, she would have seen a worried wrinkle around their eyes. But she was too excited and missed it entirely, not even noticing when her parents excused themselves halfway through the movie to put Hyacinth and Laney to bed.

The movie was nearly done when Jessie looked around and realized that only she and Orlando were there.

"Where did everyone go?"

"Your sisters were falling asleep."

"So here we were watching *Babe* when we could

have been watching a National Geographic documentary?" Jessie flicked the computer and projector off, closed the laptop, and leaned her head back. A few clouds drifted lazily in front of the moon. Footsteps creaked up the fire escape, and Jessie and Orlando turned toward the sound.

Papa appeared. "Hey. Miss Josie would like to chat with you both before bed. Can you come down?"

Orlando shot up out of the Adirondack chair. "Is she okay?"

"She's fine. Come on, let's go see her."

Orlando and Jessie glanced at each other, then grabbed the laptop and projector before silently following Papa down the fire escape. They waited for Papa to awkwardly squeeze through the second-floor window before hopping inside themselves. Jessie froze at the sight of Miss Josie's red eyes. She held a crumpled tissue in her hand.

"What's going on?" Orlando asked.

"Sit down," Miss Josie told him.

Orlando and Jessie didn't sit down. They just stood there, waiting, while Papa took a seat next to Mama and Miss Josie.

"You know I love you," Miss Josie said to Orlando. There was silence.

Miss Josie cleared her throat and began again. "I submitted paperwork for guardianship last week, and part of the application requires a home visit. When the officer came a few days ago to inspect the apartment, he said that there needs to be a separate bedroom for you."

"I don't mind sleeping on the couch," Orlando said quickly. "That's fine with me."

"The officer said I need a two-bedroom apartment," Miss Josie clarified. "I'm going to look for one, but it might take a while."

Jessie glanced around the apartment Miss Josie had lived in for decades. The furniture was perfectly arranged to fit, and every nook and cranny was filled with the things she and Mr. Jeet had collected over their lifetimes.

Orlando shook his head. "You can't move, Aunt Josie. This is your home."

"The officer gave me a week to figure things out, but I wanted to let you know what's going on. I'll do everything in my power to make sure you're cared for."

There was a long pause, then Orlando nodded. "You've done so much for me already. I'm grateful."

"You have always been a bright light for me and Mr. Jeet. We love you."

Orlando stood up and kissed Miss Josie's cheek. "I love you too," he said, then, "I've got to get up early tomorrow to train with the team and then head to the marathon route. Good night, everyone."

"Good night," Miss Josie, Mama, Papa, and Jessie said. They watched him go into the bedroom and shut the door.

"We should get going too," Mama said, standing up and giving Miss Josie a hug.

Jessie trailed behind her parents as they went downstairs to their apartment. Her parents followed her into her bedroom. Isa was still at the homecoming dance, and the room was empty and lonely.

"Are you okay, honey?" Mama asked.

Jessie shook her head. "This whole situation is wrong. He should be able to stay with Miss Josie. He should be with someone who can take great care of him. We can help Miss Josie find a two-bedroom apartment, right?"

"We could," Papa said slowly, "but it would be hard. She's lived in this building so long, and Mr. Beiderman doesn't charge her a lot of money for rent. Trying to get a bigger apartment will most likely be beyond her budget. She's also had some health challenges recently, and she worries about how long she can take care of him."

"But Orlando is no trouble," Jessie said. "He can help *her.*"

"Orlando has been taking care of his mom his entire life," Mama said. "Miss Josie thinks it's time for someone to take care of his needs for once."

Jessie's heart gave a heavy thump. "So he has to go back to Georgia?"

Papa shook his head. "We don't know yet. We have to see what happens."

Jessie crawled into bed without changing into her pajamas, buried herself in her covers, and turned toward the wall. "That's so messed up. Hasn't he been through enough?"

☼ ☼ ☼

Later that night, Jessie sent a text to Orlando.

> **JESSIE:** Thinking about you.
>
> **JESSIE:** We'll figure something out. Everything is going to be okay.

She waited for a few minutes to see if Orlando would respond, but her phone was silent. She put the phone down next to her bed and closed her eyes, suddenly exhausted.

Jessie could not understand why a person as wonderful as Orlando had to go through so much. He deserved a home. He deserved a father who would sit next to him in the hard times. He deserved three meals a day and a mom who picked up the phone when he called and a family who cheered for him from the sidelines when he ran cross-country. Jessie held all those thoughts close to her heart, wishing them into reality as she fell into a restless sleep.

Sunday, November 3

Marathon Day

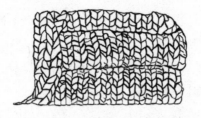

Thirty-Two

When the Vanderbeekers woke up on Sunday, the sky was gray with low-hanging clouds. It was drizzly and cold, and for once, the Vanderbeekers could sleep in. Because the marathon organizers staggered the runners' starting times, Mr. Beiderman wouldn't begin until ten thirty, which meant that if all went well, he would arrive at the first agreed-upon cheer site at 59th Street and 1st Avenue around one o'clock. After that, the Vanderbeekers would have to rush to the other two cheer locations to catch him as he passed by.

It was the last day of Daylights Saving Time—Mama and Papa's favorite day of the year—and the clocks had all been turned back the night before, so everyone had gotten an extra hour of sleep. Isa, exhausted from staying out late at the dance the night before, slept through her eight o'clock alarm, while Hyacinth woke up at six. Determined to finish Orlando's quilt, Hyacinth planned to give it to him that evening after the marathon.

Mama was the first one awake and downstairs after Hyacinth. It was just before nine o'clock, and she kissed Hyacinth's cheek on her way to the kitchen to make breakfast. Hyacinth, almost done with her quilt, got up and followed Mama. The quilt was huge and a little uneven, a natural outcome when multiple kids with varying knitting abilities contributed to the project. Hyacinth was sewing the last square to the quilt when Jessie, Oliver, Laney, and Papa tumbled down the stairs, following the scent of blueberry scones, scrambled eggs, and hash browns.

"Eat up!" Mama said as she placed an enormous bowl of fruit salad on the table.

"Did you know," Laney said as she picked up a plate and tried to separate the "good" fruit (grapes, strawberries, and blueberries) from the "yucky" fruit (honeydew and cantaloupe), "that Mr. Beiderman had to get up at five in the morning to take a bus to the starting line in Staten Island?"

"That's way early," Oliver said with a loud yawn.

"And he had to put everything except for his wallet into a clear bag that has his marathon number on it and the marathon people take it to the finish line so he doesn't have to carry it when he runs," Laney said expertly.

"I had no idea. I can't even imagine all the logistics related to such a huge event!" Mama said as she scooped a spoonful of eggs onto Laney's plate.

"I finished Orlando's quilt! It's done!" Hyacinth jumped from her seat and waved the knitted quilt in her arms.

"Yay!" cheered everyone except Jessie.

Jessie waited for her siblings to quiet down, then said, "You know that Orlando can't stay with Miss Josie, right?"

"What?" Hyacinth said. Her arms dropped and the quilt slid to the ground.

"But he just told us last night he was staying!" Oliver said.

Laney burst into tears.

Papa put an arm around Jessie. "Let's not get ahead of ourselves. We're figuring things out right now."

"We've hit an administrative hurdle," Mama added, "that we hope to have solved very soon."

"I don't want him to leave," Laney cried.

Mama held up her hands. "Listen, I know this is upsetting, but please don't worry. We're working on a solution, but right now Mr. Beiderman is expecting us to give him bananas and water on the marathon route. Let's get moving, and I promise we'll talk more about this later today."

The Vanderbeekers finished breakfast and were cleaning up the kitchen when someone pounded on the front door.

Papa opened it to find Miss Josie, out of breath and flushed.

"What's going on?" Papa said, concerned. "Is something wrong?"

"Have you seen Orlando?" she asked in a panic.

"No," Papa said, looking around. Everyone was shaking their heads.

Miss Josie's face was stricken. "He's gone."

Thirty-Three

"How do you know he's gone?" Mama asked. "I thought he was heading out early for a morning run with his cross-country team. They were going to see Mr. Beiderman on the course, right?"

"I thought so," Miss Josie said through her tears. "I didn't hear him leave this morning, so I figured he must have left early, but when I was making tea I found this note by my teacup." She handed a piece of paper to Mama.

"'Dear Aunt Josie,'" Mama read. "'Thanks for everything. I'm sorry I imposed on you for so long. Don't worry about me. I'm going home. Love, Orlando.'"

"What does that *mean?*" Oliver said. "Home is *here,* right? Or does he mean Georgia? What if he went back to the garden shed?"

Mama looked at Isa and Oliver. "Go to the garden shed. See if he's there."

They ran out the door while Mama guided Miss Josie to the couch.

"And he left his phone next to the note," Miss Josie said, holding out Orlando's phone. She was starting to sob now.

Jessie grabbed Orlando's phone from Miss Josie and turned it on. The messages she had sent last night about how everything was going to be okay were still unread.

"Why would he leave his phone?" Papa exclaimed.

"I think," Jessie said slowly, "that he felt awkward about having it because he knew you were paying for it."

"His things are gone," Miss Josie managed to say between sobs. "His backpack and most of his clothes and his toiletries as well."

"Jessie, has he contacted you at all?" Mama asked.

Jessie pulled her phone out. "No. Let me text his cross-country friends."

Mama rubbed her temples. "Who else would he talk to?"

"Maybe Mr. Beiderman?" Jessie said. "They've been spending a lot of time together."

Papa glanced at his watch. "Maybe we can catch him before his race." He took his phone from his back pocket and dialed the number. It went to voicemail.

"Mr. Beiderman was going to put his phone in a bag that the marathon people are bringing to the finish line," Laney told them. "He didn't want to run with it."

Jessie checked her phone. "I've heard back from two of the people on the cross-country team. He didn't show up for practice this morning. I remember Orlando saying the team would begin running with Mr. Beiderman starting at mile sixteen. That's the first time the runners enter Manhattan, and I think Orlando had the first shift. Maybe he'll show up there?"

Mama looked up something on her phone. "Here's

the New York City Marathon app. We can check where Mr. Beiderman is." She typed in Mr. Beiderman's marathon bib number and they all watched the little circle spin and spin until it showed his location: he had just passed mile marker three.

"He's running about ten-minute miles. At that rate, he'll cross into Manhattan in about two hours. We could try to catch him in Brooklyn and tell him to keep a lookout for Orlando on the route, but I'm not sure we could make it in time if we use the subways. And it's impossible to drive there, with all the road closures from the race."

Oliver and Isa burst through the door. "He's not in the shed," Isa reported. "There's nothing there except the gardening tools."

"Okay, people," Mama said. "We should split up. Miss Josie, why don't you make calls to everyone who might know where he is, including your folks in Georgia. Jessie, keep checking with the cross-country team. Isa, run to the high school and see if he's there. Let's convene again in forty-five minutes to debrief, and then some of us will head down to the marathon route to try to find Mr. Beiderman."

Miss Josie made call after call while Isa ran to the high school. Isa found it locked up tight with no sign of anyone there. Jessie continued to get messages from the cross-country team: none of them had heard from Orlando since the pasta dinner the night before. When it was time to leave and they still had no more information, it was decided that Miss Josie and Hyacinth would stay behind in the brownstone in case Orlando came back; everyone else would go down to the marathon route. Laney rushed around, cramming things into her pocket that she thought she might need in their search for Orlando.

Before they ran out the door, Hyacinth shoved the quilt into a bag and gave it to Jessie. "In case you find him."

Because of all the street closures, the only option to get to Midtown was the subway. Thankfully, there were no subway delays, and the Vanderbeekers got off the train at 59th Street and Lexington and ran east toward First Avenue. Papa, Jessie, and Oliver kept an eye out for Orlando among the spectators, while Mama, Isa, and Laney elbowed their way to the front of the crowd so they had an unobstructed view.

As runners went by, Laney would yell, "Have you seen Mr. B? Purple shirt? Lots of sparkles? It's an emergency!"

"Sorry, kid," a runner puffed, out of breath. "Haven't seen him."

Laney was met with lots of head shakes but many encouraging words.

"I hope you find him!" answered a person in a shirt that said "JOY" in big, blocky white letters.

"I hope everything's okay," another runner said. He was carrying a Mexican flag as he ran.

Mama kept checking and refreshing the marathon app. "He should be coming soon."

Papa and the rest of the kids returned from trying to locate Orlando in the crowd. He was nowhere to be seen.

The Vanderbeekers stared at the river of runners, but there were so many of them they were worried Mr. Beiderman had passed without their notice. Finally, one runner wearing an orange shirt that said "I'm running for Fred's Team!" heard Laney's pleas and said, "Mr. B? With the sequins?"

Laney nodded. "We need to find him!"

"I just passed a guy wearing a sparkly Mr. B shirt on the bridge. He had a leg cramp," the runner told her, jogging in place to keep her body warm. "He should be coming soon." The runner turned around and yelled to other people wearing orange shirts. "Pass the message to Mr. B that his folks are looking for him. He's wearing a purple shirt with sequins. It's an emergency."

And there, in the middle of the busiest marathon in the world, where fifty thousand runners from all over the globe were racing through the boroughs, a message was passed back from runner to runner until it reached the ears of Mr. Beiderman. He had stopped on the Queensboro Bridge to stretch out his leg cramp, but when he heard that people were looking for him and that it was an emergency he raced in their direction.

"Make way for Mr. B!" the runners around him said, clearing a path for Mr. B to get over the bridge and to the side of the street where the Vanderbeekers were looking for him.

"What happened?" Mr. Beiderman said, his worried expression transforming into panic when he saw their faces. "What's wrong?"

"Orlando's gone!" Jessie cried.

Mr. Beiderman's face went pale, and he leaned against the police barricade that separated runners from spectators. "He was supposed to meet me here, at mile sixteen. Are you sure he's not here?"

They looked around, all hoping that Orlando would come bounding out of the crowd. When he didn't, Papa quickly described what had happened the previous night.

"Has he said anything to you?" Jessie asked.

"No," Mr. Beiderman said. "This is terrible. We have to find him."

"Wait a second," Jessie said, holding her arms up. "The problem with Miss Josie's place is that she doesn't have a second bedroom, right?"

Mama, Papa, and Mr. Beiderman nodded.

"And Miss Josie is worried about her health and how that might affect her ability to take care of Orlando, right?"

The adults nodded again, confused, while Isa, Oliver, and Laney suddenly understood what Jessie was hinting at.

"That's brilliant!" Oliver exclaimed. "Why didn't I think of it?"

"A perfect solution!" Isa said.

"I love it!" Laney added.

"Love what?" Mr. Beiderman asked at the same time Papa said, "What perfect solution?"

"Well," Jessie said, "there's an apartment in our brownstone with a spare bedroom, right?"

Her siblings nodded in excitement while the adults processed the question.

"*And,*" Jessie said, her voice getting louder, "an extremely healthy adult who also happens to love Orlando lives there, right?"

"Right!" yelled Laney.

"So we think," Jessie said, looking at Mr. Beiderman, "that the answer is right here in front of us. You should be Orlando's guardian."

"Oh my gosh," breathed Mama. "That *is* perfect."

The Vanderbeekers watched for Mr. Beiderman's

reaction. He had gone utterly still, a stark contrast to the movement of the runners and spectators all around them.

The Vanderbeekers could see the exact moment that Mr. Beiderman made his decision. His posture got a little straighter, his eyes turned clear and bright, and a look of determination took over his face.

"Let's find him," Mr. Beiderman announced. "Where do you think he might have gone?"

"We checked the whole neighborhood and texted his cross-country friends," Isa reported, "and Miss Josie has called all the relatives in Georgia. No one has heard from him."

"He could have gone back to Georgia," Oliver suggested.

"Oh my gosh," Mama said, putting her hands on her face. "He went back to Georgia. By himself."

Papa grabbed his phone. "I'm going to check bus schedules." He tapped at his phone. "Buses to Atlanta left late last night and early this morning."

"Are you sure he could have gotten on a bus?" Isa asked. "How would he have enough money for a ticket?"

"I gave him some money when he moved in with Miss Josie," Mr. Beiderman said. "In case of emergencies."

"I'll call Miss Josie and see if she remembers hearing anything," Mama said. After a brief conversation on the phone, Mama hung up. "She hasn't heard anything from him since he went to bed yesterday. He could have taken a late bus last night."

"An express Greyhound bus left last night at ten thirty," Papa said. "It arrives in Atlanta tonight at eight thirty."

"I bet you anything he's on that bus," Mr. Beiderman said, grabbing Papa's phone from his hand. "We need to get to him." He looked up a number in his contacts, then put the phone to his ear and said, "Tonya, I have an emergency. I need a ticket to Atlanta today." He glanced at Jessie and then at her parents. Mama and Papa nodded. "Actually," Mr. Beiderman amended, "two tickets. One in my name and one for Jessie Vanderbeeker."

Jessie's eyes widened. "Me?" she squeaked.

While he was waiting for the flights to be booked, Mr. Beiderman covered the mouthpiece and said,

"That's my travel agent. She's going to get us on a flight that leaves at three thirty. Okay with you?"

The Vanderbeekers nodded, but they were stunned. Their neighbor, who only a few years ago refused to leave his apartment, had a travel agent now?

Mama look at Jessie. "You're okay going on an airplane?"

None of the Vanderbeeker kids had flown before, but Jessie nodded. "Yes!"

Mr. Beiderman hung up and handed the phone to Papa, but Papa shook his head.

"Take mine so you can be in contact," Papa said.

Mr. Beiderman nodded and shoved it into his pants pocket, then looked at Jessie. "Let's go! We've got a plane to catch!"

And off they went, Mr. Beiderman wearing his sparkly purple running shirt and running pants, carrying nothing but his wallet and Papa's phone, and Jessie with her phone and a knitted quilt.

It was time to bring Orlando home.

Thirty-Four

To get away from all the marathon traffic, Mr. Beiderman and Jessie had to run to the next avenue. Luckily, they were able to snag an available yellow taxi passing by. They jumped in and Mr. Beiderman directed the cabdriver to John F. Kennedy airport. The streets were crowded with cars because of the road closures from the marathon, and Mr. Beiderman kept staring at his watch and then at the sea of cars, buses, and trucks crowding the highway. Their taxi driver drove as if he were a bank robber being chased by police, weaving in and out of traffic within inches of other vehicles, jerking to a stop only when the cab was in danger of hitting pedestrians or other cars. Jessie held on to the strap by the door to keep from being thrown around the back seat. It was a harrowing ride, and when they finally got to the correct terminal, Jessie's stomach was flipping.

"It's going to be close," Mr. Beiderman said, glancing at his watch for the thousandth time right before the cab squealed to a stop at the curb. "Get ready to run." He handed the driver some of the bills from his wallet, then jumped out of the car and dashed for the entrance.

Being out in the fresh air and away from the musty cab smell perked Jessie up, and she chased Mr. Beiderman to the airline kiosk, the bag filled with Hyacinth's knitted quilt banging against her leg as she ran. Mr. Beiderman scanned his driver's license, and two boarding passes slid out into a compartment below the screen. They rushed to the security screening area. Thankfully, Mr. Beiderman had a special pass that allowed them to go through the shorter security line.

The Transportation Security Administration guy glanced at his license, looked at their boarding passes, then said, "You're going to have to run for it. I just heard them call for final boarding."

Since they had no personal items except for their wallets, phones, and the knitted blanket, they zipped through security and made a run for Gate 21. Down the long passageway filled with travelers, Jessie could see their gate. An airline agent was just about to close the doors to the jetway when Mr. Beiderman put on a burst of speed, weaving through people and luggage, his arms pumping wildly as if his life depended on getting through that door before it shut.

"Wait!" he called. "We're here! We need to get to Atlanta!"

The gate agent gestured for them to hurry. They arrived sweaty and breathless, and the agent scanned their passes and pushed them through the door before shutting and locking it. Mr. Beiderman and Jessie ran down the jet bridge, entered the plane, and squeezed through the narrow aisle as all the seated passengers silently observed Mr. B's glittery marathon shirt. They found row thirty-four and sank into their seats.

"I didn't think we were going to make it," Mr. Beiderman said, out of breath.

"Wow, Mr. B! It was like you were Usain Bolt or something," Jessie said.

Mr. Beiderman shook his head. "That's it, no more running for me. I'm done."

He leaned back and closed his eyes.

Jessie looked out the window. The airplane was moving out of the gate, and it rumbled slowly to the runway. A few minutes later, the engines fired up, the sound building in Jessie's ears. The plane began to accelerate and nose its way into the sky. Jessie looked down and watched New York City get smaller and smaller beneath her, the cars turning into ants and the buildings turning into pebbles. Then the plane broke through the clouds, the city disappeared from beneath her, and they were on their way to Atlanta.

"Mr. B?" Jessie asked.

"You know I woke up at five in the morning, right?" he said, not opening his eyes.

"What happens if we don't find Orlando in Atlanta?" she asked.

Mr. Beiderman shook his head, his eyes still closed. "Then we'll keep searching for him until we do find him."

Jessie settled back in her seat, satisfied with his answer. She would do whatever it took to find her best friend and bring him home.

✤ ✤ ✤

Jessie thought she would be too riled up to sleep, but the white noise of the jet engines and the comforting swaying motion made her drowsy. She woke up as the pilot announced their descent into Hartsfield–Jackson Atlanta International Airport. She turned her head to find Mr. Beiderman trying to cut off the sequins on his shirt with a blunt pair of children's craft scissors. When he noticed that she was awake he passed her a bottle of water and a bag of pretzels.

"You missed the drink and snack cart."

"Where did you get the scissors?" she croaked.

"The flight attendant," Mr. B said, sighing, "but they don't work. Laney must have had Hyacinth help her with the stitches. These sequins are sewn on tight."

Jessie's mouth was dry from her nap, and the water felt good going down her throat. She stretched and looked out the window to see Atlanta. A system of highways crisscrossed below her, and pretty soon she could see individual cars. Then the wheels touched the ground with a quick jolt before the plane decelerated down the runway.

It would be a couple of hours until the New York City bus arrived at the Atlanta Greyhound station, but Mr. Beiderman and Jessie were impatient to get there in case the bus got in early. They took a cab straight to the bus station, picked up some peanut butter crackers and water at the concession stand, and sat on a bench.

Jessie spent the next hour and a half observing everything around her. A big family wearing matching green shirts that said "Cohen Family Reunion!" marched through, as well as groups of weary travelers carrying an assortment of duffel bags and backpacks and rolling suitcases. Occasionally she would stand up and walk around the station. The next time she glanced at the clock, it was a few minutes before eight thirty. Mr. Beiderman nudged her.

"The bus is pulling in," he told her, pointing to the door where the lights of a bus were shining through the glass.

Jessie jumped up and ran to the door. She let herself outside and stood by the front of the bus, waiting for the driver to open the doors. Finally, a long line of tired travelers began disembarking. There were people of all ages, some who looked as if they were college students and others who looked Miss Josie's age. After they exited, they went to the side of the bus, where the driver was yanking suitcases and duffel bags from the storage compartment and piling them up on the ground. A few kids wearing pajamas and holding stuffed animals also came off the bus. Soon all of the bags were gone, and the travelers dispersed.

"He's not here," Jessie said to Mr. Beiderman, her eyes filling with tears. "We were wrong."

"Maybe he took the later bus," Mr. Beiderman told her, putting an arm around her shoulders. "Or maybe he used a different bus company. It's okay. We won't stop until we find him."

The bus driver got back on the bus to move it to the depot, and Jessie and Mr. Beiderman turned around to go back into the station and figure out what to do next.

Mr. Beiderman opened the door for Jessie, but before she went through, she heard someone call her name.

"Jessie? Mr. Beiderman?"

Jessie swiveled to see Orlando in the doorway of the bus. He was rumpled, as if he had just woken up, and when his eyes connected with Jessie's, he rubbed his face as if he had seen a ghost.

"Orlando!" Jessie rushed forward and hugged him.

"What are you doing here?" Orlando said, dazed.

"We're here to bring you back to Harlem," Mr. Beiderman said.

Orlando shook his head. "I don't want Aunt Josie to move for me. It's too much."

Mr. Beiderman nodded. "You're right. It would be too much for Miss Josie to move. She's also getting older, and she's going to need more help in the near future."

"So . . . why are you here?"

"Because," Mr. Beiderman said, "you belong with us. We want you to come home."

Jessie waited for Mr. Beiderman's next words. The bus had left and the lot was dark and quiet. The overhead lights buzzed quietly, illuminating the two people in front of her, their silhouettes tall and strong despite what both of them had gone through in their lives.

Mr. Beiderman put his hand on Orlando's shoulder, and when he spoke, his voice was so quiet that Jessie had to lean in to hear. "Almost ten years ago, my wife and daughter were killed when a car hit them a few blocks away from our home. It took me many years to learn how to love again, and it was mostly because of the Vanderbeekers that I found the courage. And when I met you, I came to love you, too. We both know what it means to lose the people closest to us. I believe that loss has connected us in deep ways."

Orlando nodded, his face cast in shadow as he looked down at the ground. Jessie wished she could see his expression.

"But, Orlando," Mr. Beiderman went on, "our stories collided for a reason. When I heard you were missing, I was terrified. And when I felt that fear, it made me realize how much you mean to me and how much I want us to navigate life together . . . if you'll agree."

Orlando stared at him, confused.

Mr. Beiderman shoved his hands in his pockets.

"I want to be your legal guardian. I have that second bedroom that we can make into your room. You can have your own space. I know it's a lot to think about," Mr. Beiderman continued quickly, "and I know you have your aunt here in Georgia who you can stay with, but if you want to come back to Harlem, I would consider it a privilege to be your guardian. Just know that I'm behind any decision you make—"

"I want that," Orlando said, his words coming out in a quick jumble as he looked up at Mr. Beiderman. "I want to come back, if you're sure about the guardian stuff."

"I am absolutely sure," Mr. Beiderman said. "But if I become your guardian, that means you're stuck with me. Forever. Are you okay with that?"

Orlando smiled. "I'm okay with that."

Thirty-Five

Mr. Beiderman and Jessie returned to the airport, this time with Orlando. They were able to get on a late-night flight to New York City, but they had a couple of hours before the plane left, so they sat at an airport restaurant, ate sandwiches and fries, and made phone calls. The first one was to Miss Josie.

"I have been waiting and waiting for you to call!" Miss Josie exclaimed over speakerphone when she answered. "Please tell me you found Orlando."

"We did," Jessie said, and Orlando said, "Hi, Aunt Josie."

"Don't you ever, ever, *ever* do that to us again, you hear?" Miss Josie said. "You took five years off my life, and at my age those are years I can't be giving up. Honey, you know I love you and would move the moon and stars for you, right?"

Orlando tried to say something, but Miss Josie went on to tell them how she knew they had found him when Billie Holiday crawled out from her hiding spot under the couch and started wagging her tail, rolling on her back, and eating without any prompting.

"Dogs know things," Miss Josie finished.

After they hung up with Miss Josie, they called Mama and Papa and texted the track team. Everyone was thrilled that they were coming home. Then it was time to turn off their phones and get on the plane.

Jessie sat in the middle of the row, between Mr. Beiderman and Orlando. She spread Hyacinth's knitted quilt so it protected them from the cold air blowing from the vents above them. Orlando picked up a corner of the blanket and examined what looked like a fabric tag. Jessie saw that Hyacinth had sewn on a tag that said "Property of Orlando Stewart" along with the address of the brownstone.

Then the engines came to life, and all three of them immediately dozed off under the cozy quilt as the plane rose into the sky. When they woke up, it was two in the morning in New York City.

Sleepy and travel worn, the three got off the plane and headed toward the exit. They entered an empty passageway that led to the taxi stand, but before they could take the escalator down to the street, they turned a corner and were met by a deafening roar.

A crowd of people was jumping and cheering and waving sticks attached to long ribbons. In front of the crowd were the Vanderbeekers, holding up a huge, glittery sign that said "Welcome Home, Orlando!"

Jessie, shocked at the sight, dropped the bag holding the quilt. Her whole family was there, as well as Miss Josie, Mr. Jones the postman, Coach Mendoza, Allegra, Herman, Angie, Jimmy L, and the entire track team plus their coach.

Jessie looked at Orlando. His jaw had dropped, and then his mouth spread into a big grin.

"Party in the middle of the night!" Oliver yelled from behind the banner.

And then the crowd ran toward Jessie, Orlando, and Mr. Beiderman, streamers and banners waving, smothering the travelers with hugs and kisses and love. Laney put medals made from red-white-and-blue ribbon and chocolate coins wrapped in gold foil around everyone's necks, and Hyacinth took fistfuls of confetti from her pocket and threw it with abandon. Oliver, who had somehow convinced the marathon organizers to give him two of the foil space blankets they give only to marathon finishers, wrapped those around Orlando and Mr. Beiderman, while Jessie and Isa cheered so loudly that a Transportation Security Agency employee had to come over and ask them to quiet down.

Three miles away in Harlem, Billie Holiday barked her high, clear bark, alerting the rest of the pets that all was well. Franz belted out a long, low howl, and Paganini raced around the living room, jumping with glee. Tuxedo and George Washington woke up, straightened their hind legs and arched their backs, then settled back down into their warm sleeping spots, their purrs rumbling satisfaction at the world being right again. The chickens, perched on their roost in the coop, ruffled their feathers in contentment before drifting back to sleep.

And the brownstone creaked with happiness as it settled into its foundation, the weathervane spinning for joy at the news, as it waited for its occupants to make their way home.

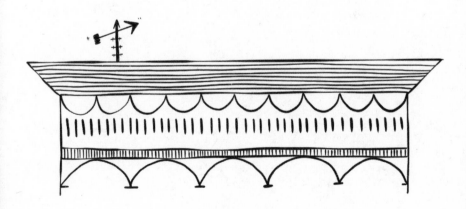

Acknowledgments

It is always a privilege and joy to work with Ann Rider. I treasure her insights, thoughtful comments, and love for golden retrievers and mukluks. Huge thanks to Tara Shanahan, the absolute best publicist in the world. Much love to the entire HMH team: Natalie Fondriest for the beautiful book design, Katya Longhi for the gorgeous cover, Jennifer Thermes for the map endpapers, and Catherine Onder, Mary Wilcox, John Sellers, Mary Magrisso, Candace Finn, Lisa DiSarro, Amanda Acevedo, Alia Almeida, all the HMH sales reps, Elizabeth Agyemang, Emily Andrukaitis, and Colleen Fellingham. I am so grateful for all the support and Vanderbeekers love.

Huge thanks to Ginger Clark for being the best

advocate and for sending snacks in troubled times. Lots of chocolate caramel cookies to Holly Frederick for being an awesome friend, neighbor, and film agent, and many thanks to Nicole M. Eisenbraun and Madeline R. Travis for all their hard work and support.

Librarians, teachers, and booksellers are national treasures and deserve palaces and an endless supply of cookies. I am grateful for all the ways they share their love of reading with young people.

Hugs to Amy Poehler, Kim Lessing, Matt Murray, and the Paper Kite team!

One of the best parts about being a writer is being surrounded by compassionate and creative colleagues in the Kid Lit community. I am grateful for all of them (too many to name!). Special thanks to Lauren Hart, Laura Shovan, Casey Lyall, Margaret Dilloway, Timanda Wertz, and Janet Johnson for their feedback on an early draft of this book.

Lots of love to Lauren Hart, Emily Rabin, Katie Graves-Abe, Harrigan Bowman, Janice Nimura, the Glaser family, and the Dickinson family for being wonderful, amazing people. A special shout-out to the communities that have inspired and encouraged me, including the Town School, Book Riot, Read-Aloud Revival, the New York Society Library, the New York Public Library, All Angels' Church, and my Harlem neighbors.

During the finishing stages of this book, I was sheltering at home with my family due to a pandemic. Many thanks to health care workers for keeping us safe and to my family for giving me the time and space to write. If I had to be stuck in a tiny apartment with anyone in the world, it would have to be Dan, Kaela, and Lina. I love them so much!

Don't Miss More
Vanderbeekers Adventures!

"Delightful and heartwarming."
—*New York Times Book Review*

★ "A pitch-perfect debut. . . . Highly recommended."
—*School Library Journal*, starred review

★ "Few families in children's literature are as engaging or amusing as the Vanderbeekers. . . . Wildly entertaining."
—*Booklist*, starred review

"Utterly enchanting."
—Linda Sue Park, Newbery medalist

A Junior Library Guild Selection
A *New York Times* Bestseller

"Timeless."
—*Horn Book*

"Glaser at her best."
—*Booklist*

"An excellent seqeul."
—*School Library Journal*

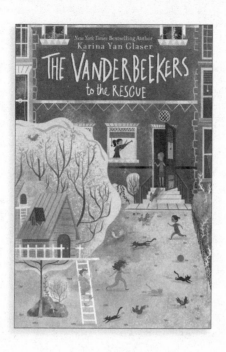

A Junior Library Guild Selection
A *Publishers Weekly* Bestseller

"Once again, Glaser produces a charming
novel reminiscent of classic and contemporary
family story mainstays . . . but she adds depth with
racial diversity, evocative city details, and complex
socioeconomic issues."
—*Kirkus Reviews*

"Almost a case study in why these kinds of series are
so captivating for young readers. . . . Heartfelt."
—*New York Times Book Review*

Look out for a new
Vanderbeekers novel in
Fall 2021!